Overflow

- a novel -

Suzanne Staton

This novel is a work of fiction. Any references to real people, events, establishments, organizations or locales are intended only to give the fiction a sense of reality and authenticity and are used fictitiously. All other names, characters and places, and all dialogue and incidents portrayed in this book are the product of the author's imagination.

Copyright © 2015 Suzanne Staton

All rights reserved. No part of this book may be used or reproduced in any manner whatsoever without written permission except in the case of brief quotations embodied in crucial articles and reviews.

The map on pages iv-v is used courtesy of the University of Texas Libraries, The University of Texas at Austin. Back cover image is part of the Library of Congress Prints and Photographs Division Repository, dedicated to the public domain under a CC0 license.

ISBN-10: 0692560580
ISBN-13: 978-0692560587

For Jonathan Dean, my biggest and always steadfast supporter.

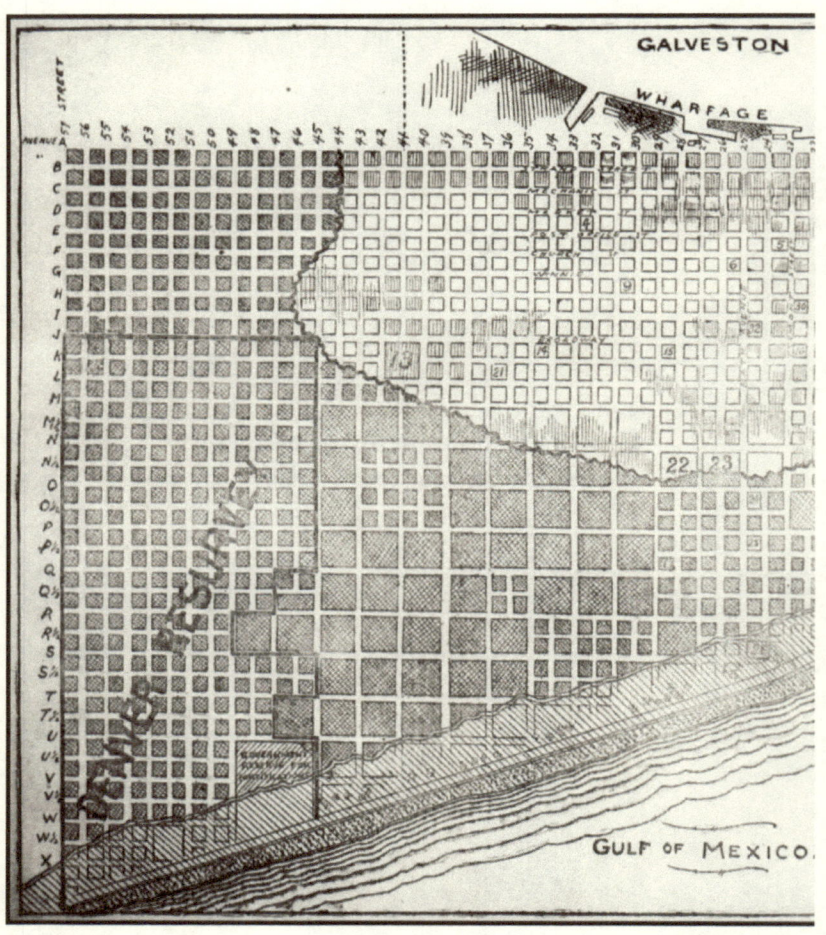

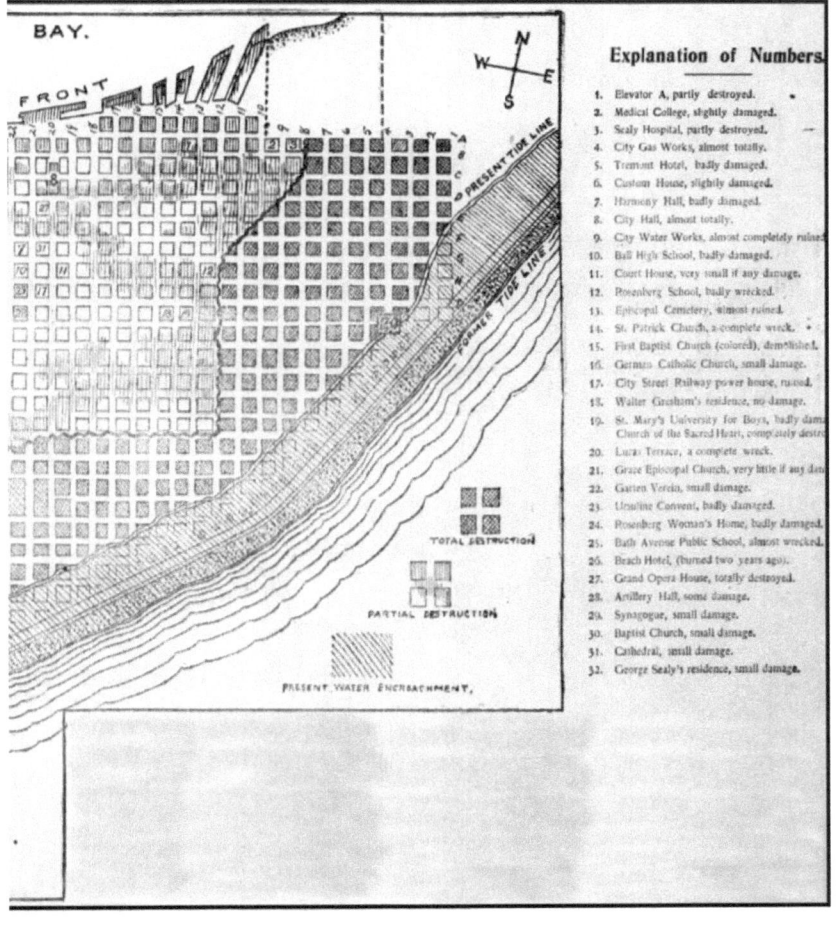

BAY.

FRONT

PRESENT TIDE LINE

FORMER TIDE LINE

TOTAL DESTRUCTION

PARTIAL DESTRUCTION

PRESENT WATER ENCROACHMENT.

Explanation of Numbers.

1. Elevator A, partly destroyed.
2. Medical College, slightly damaged.
3. Sealy Hospital, partly destroyed.
4. City Gas Works, almost totally.
5. Tremont Hotel, badly damaged.
6. Custom House, slightly damaged.
7. Harmony Hall, badly damaged.
8. City Hall, almost totally.
9. City Water Works, almost completely ruined.
10. Ball High School, badly damaged.
11. Court House, very small if any damage.
12. Rosenberg School, badly wrecked.
13. Episcopal Cemetery, almost ruined.
14. St. Patrick Church, a complete wreck.
15. First Baptist Church (colored), demolished.
16. German Catholic Church, small damage.
17. City Street Railway power house, ruined.
18. Walter Gresham's residence, no damage.
19. St. Mary's University for Boys, badly dama[...]
   Church of the Sacred Heart, completely destro[...]
20. Lucas Terrace, a complete wreck.
21. Grace Episcopal Church, very little if any dam[...]
22. Garten Verein, small damage.
23. Ursuline Convent, badly damaged.
24. Rosenberg Woman's Home, badly damaged.
25. Bath Avenue Public School, almost wrecked.
26. Beach Hotel, (burned two years ago).
27. Grand Opera House, totally destroyed.
28. Artillery Hall, some damage.
29. Synagogue, small damage.
30. Baptist Church, small damage.
31. Cathedral, small damage.
32. George Sealy's residence, small damage.

V

PROLOGUE

SEPTEMBER 8, 1900

Haydn Winters stood on a dune, looking out at the rising sea. The previous night had been hot, but that wasn't the reason he'd been unable to sleep. At first light, he had walked to the beach to relieve some of his restlessness, but as the sun rose, he had become more than just restless. He was uneasy.

The sky bloomed a bright pink, with wispy clouds reflecting light and color across the horizon like fish scales. It was beautiful, but it seemed at odds with what was happening in the water.

There was a north wind, which should mean a low tide, but instead the swells seemed to be growing. How they were doing so in the face of the opposing wind, Haydn couldn't understand. The waves were turning brown from the sand kicking up underneath them, and they didn't just seem to be crashing on the beach—they seemed to be attacking it.

As the pink color faded in the sky, black clouds began to fill in, sinking very low, as if they were going to smother him. It all felt very menacing.

But then, he might just be imposing his own angst upon the weather. Overflows happened on Galveston all the time. But days like today didn't come every day. Today would be momentous. Today, he would learn the truth.

He had lain awake all night, rehearsing what he would say. He had chased the words around in his mind, over and over, roiling with anticipation, uncertainty and, finally, determination.

Like the waves, his impatience had swelled until he felt like he might explode. He was ready for whatever squall would come from the confrontation. It was time.

CHAPTER 1

FEBRUARY 27, 1900

Bracing against the cold morning breeze, Haydn Winters tugged the collar of his dark grey overcoat around his neck. The Galveston sun peeked above the horizon, and the pale orange light spreading across the sky gave false promise of a warm day.

Even on an island in the Gulf of Mexico, February could be uncomfortably cold, and Haydn longed for his bed. It had been all he could do to leave it this morning. He had hidden, burrowed under the covers, hoping the world would forget about him.

But the Winters' head house servant, Jefferson Cole, had come into the room to coax alive a flame in the fireplace, as he did every morning during cold months, and Haydn knew he would have to get up.

When Jefferson left, Haydn told himself he should get moving. But the minutes ticked by with him still cocooned in blankets. As each minute passed, his anxiety inched up a notch. He knew the time was approaching when he could no longer avoid starting this day—this damned day that would lead to this damned evening. He knew that as soon as he left the warm confines of his bed, he would begin hurtling toward this evening, and that he did not want to face.

Finally, he sighed and admitted that an even more frightening thought was having to face his father if he was late for work. So he pushed off the covers.

He now hunched his shoulders as he moved along the sidewalk, trying to tuck his own body heat into himself. The effect was that his 5-foot-11-inch frame looked a couple of inches shorter. His brown eyes were trained on the ground, and his chin was pressed toward his chest, aiming downward a perfectly shaped nose.

Brown hair peeked out from under a dark, felt Homburg hat, which to his chagrin was not quite covering his ears. On his right ear lobe was a freckle that he rubbed when he was nervous. At the moment, however, his hands were plunged deep into the pockets of his overcoat. Without his gloves, which he had forgotten on a walnut side table in the front hall at home, no amount of apprehension could have coaxed his hands out of the warm wool of his coat pockets.

Haydn took his usual route to his father's bank, where he'd worked for the past nine months. It was a straight walk six blocks north from the Winters' house, dubbed Painter House by his maternal grandfather, George Painter, who had built the home at 21st Street and Broadway, to the bank at 22nd and Mechanic. Haydn could walk the route with his eyes closed, and was practically doing that now, except that he was jogging, partially to keep warm and partially to make up time.

With his head down, Haydn crossed Market Street. "Just one more block to go," he said to himself, then ran smack into a brown, hairy wall. His feet stumbled to a stop as a horse blew a startled breath of steam from its nose and jerked sideways.

"Whoa, there!" a voice called out. A man holding reins attached to the horse gently steadied the animal. The horse was pulling a cart loaded with groceries, and the cart's driver pulled to a stop, then looked at Haydn. "Well, good morning, Mr. Winters!"

"Good morning, Mr. Mills. I'm sorry I scared Goliath," Haydn said and patted the horse's neck.

"He'll survive. He's a brute of a horse, but I declare he starts at the drop of a hat."

"And at a 170-pound man running into him," Haydn said. "I'm surprised to see you at this hour. Deliveries so early?"

"Yes, sir," the driver nodded. "There are parties all over town tonight, and if I don't have these groceries delivered by noon, I'll be the first course!" The man laughed.

"Oh, of course, the parties," Haydn said. "This looks like a fine load, Mr. Mills. I hope some of it is destined for the Martin home."

"Be assured of that, Mr. Winters."

Haydn pulled a pocket watch from the folds of his coat.

"I'm afraid I'm running a little behind schedule," he said. *Fifteen minutes*, he noted with concern.

"Well, then I won't keep either of us," Mr. Mills said. "Have a glorious morning! And Happy Fat Tuesday!" He jerked the reins to urge his horse into motion. Haydn had no chance to answer as Mr. Mills steered his cart noisily down the street.

Haydn wondered if Barton Mills would be attending any parties tonight. With four children to feed on a deliveryman's salary, he was sure Barton didn't have the money to throw one. Then again, parties closer to the beach were simpler affairs than the one he'd be attending at the Martin home.

The Martins were Galveston royalty and attending their annual Mardi Gras ball confirmed a guest's status as part of the city's royal court. Haydn's mother, Mildred

Painter Winters, insisted the family go every year. This year the ball would be an extension of the Martins' lavish New Year's Eve celebration, which had been especially festive. It wasn't every year the world ushered in a new century, and Galvestonians intended the first year of the 20th century to be a year to remember.

A few minutes later, Haydn pushed through the doors of Galveston Fidelity Bank. Joseph Winters looked up from his desk located to the right of the door. When Haydn met his eyes, his father extracted a pocket watch from his vest, glanced pointedly at the time, then replaced the watch.

Haydn removed his coat and hat and hung them on a coat rack next to his father's desk. He smoothed his hair, which was parted slightly off-center, and walked toward two teller windows that faced the front door.

A young man entered the lobby from the vault at the rear of the bank. He was tall and unusually handsome, with dark blonde hair parted so far to the left that a wave formed across his forehead. He had the same perfect nose as Haydn, but a stronger, square jawline, striking blue eyes that sloped downward at the edges, and lips that curled upward at the ends in a perpetual impish grin.

"Aha! He joins us!" the young man said breaking into a broad smile.

"Good morning, George," Haydn said.

"So tell me, little brother. Were you up late last night

planning for tonight's festivities? Were you deciding which of the lovelies to dance with at the Martins' or planning to sneak off to the alleys on Post Office Street?"

He bumped shoulders with Haydn.

"I believe Post Office Street is more your speed," Haydn said, a smile creeping onto his face.

"Why, I don't know what you mean! Am I to be harassed because I have mail on occasion?"

Haydn laughed, and it felt good. Post Office Street was rightly named as the street on which one could find the city's post office—the state's first post office, in fact. However, it was also where one could find the city's red-light district.

The district, which ran along Post Office Street between 25th Street and 29th Street, consisted of two-story, narrow-frame houses with front porches that did not actually sport red light bulbs, but their inhabitants provided the same services as those in red-light districts in other big cities around the globe. The district's houses of prostitution and saloons fed the city's appetites for sex, alcohol, gambling and drugs.

"I'm not interested in mail," Haydn said, raising his eyebrows at his brother.

"That'll be enough," Mr. Winters looked up from the papers he was working on long enough to give the boys a disapproving look. "A customer could walk through that door any moment, and—"

"And we must instill confidence from the moment they enter Galveston Fidelity," George said, standing up straight and placing his hand over his heart with the last two words.

Haydn stifled a laugh, and his father looked at him over his glasses.

"I'm sorry, father," George said, placing his hands in trouser pockets, but his grin suggested the words were more a deference to his father than an expression of remorse. "You're right. We won't talk about mail anymore."

Mr. Winters turned his attention back to his papers, and George seated himself at a desk near the vault. Haydn walked behind one of the teller windows and began to count money that George had laid out in the window's drawer for the day's transactions.

As he counted, a small, graying man with a neatly trimmed beard and a slight stoop entered the building and hung his coat on Mr. Winters' coat rack.

"Good morning, Stefan," Mr. Winters said without looking up.

"Good morning, Mr. Winters," the man said with a trace of a German accent and a slight bow.

Stefan took his place behind the other teller window and began to count his cash drawer. Joseph demanded his sons be at the bank at 8:00 a.m. to prepare for the day's work, but Stefan was not due until 9:00 a.m. He always arrived early, though.

Haydn had worked next to Stefan since he'd been at the bank, after he returned from a year abroad that many Galveston society youths took upon graduating high school. He was glad to work with the older man, whom he had known his whole life and considered a surrogate grandfather. Stefan was far more accommodating when Haydn had questions than either George or his father. His father looked aggravated when Haydn didn't know something, and George teased him. Stefan, though, would simply show him how to do something or explain the bank's operations without judgment.

"All your bills—they face the same direction?" he asked Haydn.

"Stefan Roemer, you ask me that every morning," Haydn said in mock exasperation. He smiled, though, to be sure Stefan knew he was kidding. "Yes, my bills are all face up. 'Easy to see and easy to count.' You've taught me well."

* * *

At the Winters' home, Mildred spoke with Jefferson about the family's preparations for the Martins' ball.

"The family will need to eat dinner earlier than usual, so be sure Elinor knows that, Jefferson. And please have all of our clothes for the ball cleaned and pressed and laid out no later than four o'clock," Mildred said.

Mildred knew that the family had the same schedule on all party days, and there were many of those, but she felt it was important to reiterate her expectations to staff. "It's going to take some time to style Margaret's hair, so I want Sallie to help with that in the afternoon. And be sure that you wash the carriage and groom the horses," she said.

"Yes, ma'am," Jefferson replied.

"That'll be all for now. I'll let you know if I need anything else."

"Yes, ma'am." Jefferson said and bowed slightly, then left the room.

Mildred could hear low murmurs as Jefferson spoke with his wife, Elinor, the family's cook. She presumed he was clarifying the day's schedule with Elinor, and she wondered if she should have been more specific on a time for Sallie to help Margaret with her hair.

Jefferson's daughter Sallie helped with household chores, particularly when it came to the Winters' only daughter, Margaret. Sallie was the same age as Margaret. In fact, she'd been born just one month before Margaret and had lived her entire life on the Winters estate.

The Winters family provided living quarters for the Coles on the back of their property, and Mildred occasionally reminded them of this generosity. However, when she did, she left out the fact that the free room and board also meant the family was available to the Winters 24 hours a day. Most days, Mildred preferred the family to have its privacy after dinner, so the Coles generally were not needed at the main house in the evenings. But party days were an exception.

Tonight, they would need Jefferson to drive the family to the party, wait in the host's kitchen with the other servants, then take the family home at the end of the night. The family would leave for the Martins' ball just after
7:00 p.m. and would not return until well after midnight.

As Mildred listened to Jefferson and Elinor's voices, too low for her to hear exactly what they were saying, she wondered if Elinor and Sallie ever used the house when the family was away at social functions. She imagined Elinor listening to her phonograph and Sallie using Margaret's bathtub. There had never been any evidence that the women did any such thing, and suddenly Margaret felt uncomfortable for thinking that they might. Sometimes she had thoughts that she couldn't account for, and that unsettled her.

She shook her head, as if to throw off the unwarranted thoughts, and went to the library to see if any correspondence required her attention.

CHAPTER 2

FEBRUARY 27, 1900

Mildred spent most of the afternoon checking on preparations for the party and planning her social calls for the rest of the week. She could only think of one friend who would want to receive visitors tomorrow on Ash Wednesday, so her other calls would have to be made later in the week, and she'd have to leave some time to be home herself to receive callers. That meant some tight scheduling. She looked at her list to see who might be expendable.

When she was satisfied with her list and had checked that preparations were under way for that night, she retired to the drawing room to listen to her phonograph and rest for the Martins' party. The phonograph was one of the new models that used flat discs instead of cylinders. Joseph had not seen the point in replacing a perfectly good cylinder phonograph, but Mildred had insisted that the new kind would suit them better. She talked about it incessantly until Joseph told her he simply refused to hear another word on the matter. Mildred took that as acceptance and purchased the new machine.

Joseph never acknowledged the purchase, which made him the only one relieved of the duty of complimenting Mildred on it, since she played it for all of her visitors. When she first got it, she always played the music just a bit too loud so she would have to remark on the volume and go to the machine to turn it down. The walk over to the machine and back gave her callers the opportunity to politely remark on the instrument, which they unfailingly did.

But one afternoon at a card game, Mildred overheard some ladies at another table joking that those new flat-disc phonographs would be nice if only the volume wasn't always so loud at first. She glanced over at the table and saw one of the ladies look at her as they laughed. After that, she didn't play it for visitors anymore.

As evening fell, Mildred found herself rushing around trying to get ready for the Martin's party. She was frustrated that Elinor seemed to constantly be occupied with busy work instead of whatever Mildred needed done.

Despite the challenges, she managed to get ready on time, though it had meant not eating dinner.

She now stood in the foyer, fussing with her hair and waiting for her family to assemble so they could ride to the party together. Sallie passed behind the stairs.

"Is Miss Margaret ready?" Mildred called out.

"No, ma'am. She's still gettin' dressed," Sallie replied.

"Then what are you doing downstairs? Why aren't you helping her?" Mildred's feet hurt from the new shoes she'd bought for the party, but she refused to sit lest she wrinkle her dark blue satin and velvet dress. She had pondered earlier if there was a way to ride in the carriage without sitting. After all, it was only five blocks to the Martin home, Casa Isla. But she couldn't think of a way. Sallie looked pained.

"She told me she didn't need my help, Missus."

"I see," Mildred said, whirling toward the stairs and mounting the first step purposefully.

"Mother, leave Margaret be," George said, appearing from the parlor holding a short glass with ice and brown liquid. Sallie slipped behind the staircase into a short hallway that led to the kitchen. "She'll be down soon enough."

"Soon enough won't do," Mildred said, reaching the fifth step. "I will not be late to the Martins."

"Why not?" George asked. "You think they won't let you in if you miss the top of the hour?"

Mildred turned and shook her finger at him. "You may not care what people think, but I will not have this family look like peasants, showing up willy-nilly, whenever the mood strikes. Someone in this family has to care about appearances. The Martins would never show up late to a party, so by God, neither will we."

"By God?" George raised his eyebrows. "What if God wants us to be late? Maybe there's going to be a fire, and everyone is going to perish, and he wants us to be late to spare us so that we can carry on Galveston society after they're all gone. Maybe Margaret is just fulfilling the Lord's wishes."

"George!" Mildred's face was red, and she was squeezing her fists.

"Has anyone seen my gloves?" Margaret's voice floated down as she descended the staircase. Mildred swiveled in her direction.

"They're in your drawer, where they always are," Mildred said through gritted teeth.

"Where's Sallie? She can find them for me," Margaret said. She primped her hair, which was piled in blonde curls on top of her head. She wore a light green satin dress with lace covering her throat and the top of her bosom. At 17, she was the youngest of the Winters children. Her blue eyes were a copy of her brother George's, and they flashed as she spoke. She turned her attention to her brother.

"Oh George! You look lovely—positively regal." Margaret swished past her mother, who was still standing on the fifth step.

"As do you, my dear," George said with a bow. "You'll be engaged by the end of the evening."

"Dear Lord, let's hope not," Margaret said and smoothed her dress. "Are we ready, then?"

"Except for your gloves," said George. He drained his glass and set it on the sideboard in the foyer.

"I'll get them," Mildred said and stomped up the stairs. When she got to the top, she heard George tell Margaret, "You really shouldn't torture her like that."

"I don't know what you're talking about," Margaret said.

"Of course not." George said. Mildred shook her head and retrieved the gloves. She returned to the foyer.

"Well, where is everyone?" Margaret asked. "Mother, from the way you carried on, you'd think the world had stopped spinning, waiting on me. But Haydn and Father aren't even here."

"Father has gone to bring the carriage around, and I don't know where Hy is," George said, using the nickname he had given his brother when Haydn was just a baby. Haydn's brother and friends used it, but Mildred and Joseph steadfastly refused.

The three put on their coats and stepped on to the front porch, where Haydn was standing, stroking the head of a dog that leaned against his leg.

"There you are," George said. "What are you doing out here? It's freezing!"

"Just waiting for Father."

"Well good Lord, man, don't look so downtrodden," George said, elbowing him. "You look positively regal, you know."

"Don't make fun of me, George!" Margaret slapped his shoulder with her fan.

Haydn patted the dog's shoulder and looked uncertainly at his brother and sister, who laughed but didn't seem to be laughing at him.

"That beast is getting hair on your pants. Shoo!" Mildred waved at the dog, who did not leave, but pressed harder against Haydn.

"He's alright, Mother," Haydn said. "Aren't you, Buddy?" The dog looked up at him with big, dark eyes.

"What is your obsession with that dog?" Mildred frowned.

"It's not an obsession," Haydn rolled his eyes. "It's called affection. I'm hardly the first person to ever have a pet."

"Just make sure he stays out of the house," Mildred said, giving the animal a wide berth as she passed.

"You don't have to say that every time you see him."

Mildred glared at the dog. It tucked its tail underneath itself and lay down behind a large potted plant, out of her sight.

The carriage pulled under the porte-cochere and up to the front steps with Jefferson perched on the driver's bench. Mr. Winters stepped out of the cab and helped his family one-by-one into the vehicle. When the cab door closed, Mildred heard Jefferson shake the reins and the carriage pulled into motion.

"I can't believe we're going to arrive in this old thing," Margaret complained.

"Old thing? We just bought this carriage a year ago," Mildred protested.

"The Martins have one of those new horseless carriages."

"Those contraptions are uncivilized," Mildred said. "And they're dangerous."

"What's so civilized about what our horse leaves in the street?"

"Not another word, Margaret. You sound like a common shop girl."

"Couldn't she be a barmaid, Mother?" George asked. "I'm empty."

"Oh, sir, let me get ya another," Margaret said, affecting an Irish accent. "And shall I tie your shoes, too?"

"That's enough," Mildred said. Haydn grinned and Joseph shook his head, allowing a small smile.

The carriage pulled up to the front door of Casa Isla,

the Victorian mansion built in 1875 by John Mason Martin. Martin had made a fortune trading cotton and investing in railroads and shipping. Mildred's father had been John's banker, and at one time, her father had encouraged her to marry John's son, Calvin. They would have been *the* society couple, but before the match could be arranged, Mildred met Joseph. Calvin certainly seemed happy with his wife Annabell, so Mildred told herself that it had all worked out for the best.

When Joseph put his hand out to help her out of the carriage, she did her best to hide a small sigh, then made her way down the steps and smoothed her dress.

Margaret hopped out of the carriage and swept past Mildred. She entered the front door, ignoring a greeting from a doorman stationed on the front porch. She handed her coat to a servant in the front foyer, then stopped to take stock of her hair in a mirror. In the reflection, she saw Annabell Martin approaching. When she turned back, Annabell took her hands and opened her arms wide.

"Oh, my dear, you look simply exquisite," Annabell said.

"Thank you, Mrs. Martin," Margaret said and smiled.

The front door pushed open with a woosh.

"Margaret, what are you—," Mildred said, then stopped herself as she caught sight of Annabell. She smiled and continued, "Margaret, darling, you should've let me come in first. It's not ladylike to rush into a room like a dervish."

Margaret just smiled at her.

"Mildred, your dress is just beautiful," Annabell said. "And where are those handsome sons of yours?"

"Right behind us," Mildred said, her hand absently smoothing the front her dress. "I don't know what takes them so long."

The men entered the foyer, and Annabell greeted them. She then ushered the family into the brightly lit and lushly decorated ballroom to the right of the great hall.

Margaret immediately peeled off to join a group of friends standing at a bay window that looked out over the mansion's front porch and lawn, allowing them to see, and be seen by, arriving guests.

"Finally!" one of the girls said to Margaret as she sat down on the window seat. "I thought you'd never get here. I'm so bored."

"It's just getting started, Emma," Margaret said. "How bored can you be?"

"Her corset is too tight, so she can't eat, and she's grumpy," said another girl.

"I'll show you how grumpy I am," Emma said.

"Don't get too worked up or you'll pass out," Margaret said. "Besides, you look too pretty to have a frown on your face."

"Thank you," Emma said and smiled.

Margaret surveyed the room. A temporary wall of smilax screened musicians from the view of guests, who seemed to be enjoying the music but weren't dancing. A bank of potted palms provided a backdrop for the refreshment table along the west wall, and arrangements of violets, narcissus and hyacinths brightened tables around the room. The fireplace mantle was adorned with roses and potted azaleas, and the room's chandeliers were draped with garlands of smilax.

A large, gilded mirror was positioned over the fireplace, reflecting the activity in the room and making the space seem even larger, and a climbing fern hung as a garland between a chandelier over the fireplace and the mirror.

"Can you imagine having your debut here?" one of the girls asked.

"I'd rather have it at the Artillery Club," said Emma. "That's more traditional than having it at home, even if home is Casa Isla."

"How about not having it at all?" asked Margaret.

"Are you going to go on about that again?" asked Emma.

"I'm serious," said Margaret. "It's humiliating."

"If humiliating is a new dress and big party with me at the center of things, I'll stand for the humiliation," said Emma.

The girls laughed. Emma laughed then winced. "I

think this thing is actually getting tighter," she said and fingered the corset through her dress.

"You know what I mean," Margaret said. "The whole exercise is just a signal to all the men and their eager parents that you're available for marriage. 'Come and get it!' Well, I'm not getting married, so I see no reason to parade myself for a bunch of overheated men."

"Margaret, shhhh!" said one of the girls, looking around. "Someone will hear you."

"So what if they do?" Margaret said. She was exasperated. She'd known these girls her whole life. They'd played together, gone to school together, gone to parties together, and she couldn't understand how not one of them shared her reluctance to become someone else's property.

"Margaret, that kind of talk was all well and good for stirring things up when we were little girls," Emma said. "But we're ladies now. You can't keep saying things like that, or people are going to believe you really feel that way."

"Yes," said one of the other girls. "I mean, of course you're going to get married. What would you do if you didn't?"

"Plenty!" Margaret said. "I could paint for one thing."

"Are you still doing that?" one of the girls asked. "You know that's not appropriate for a woman in your position."

"You sound like my mother," Margaret said with pursed lips. "Besides, I could do other things, too. I could work with charities. I could help at St. Mary's Orphanage or serve on the Audubon Society's governing board. There are all kinds of things I could do as a woman in my position. And not one of them would involve giving my money to some man who would then think he could tell me what to do."

"Well, I wouldn't mind one of your brothers telling me what to do for the next 50 years," said Emma, grinning. "That George is a dream, and Haydn just makes you want to take him in your arms and make it all better."

"Oh, that sad face," Margaret said. She picked a flower from an arrangement on a table next to her. "I'm so tired of looking at that. If he doesn't stop pining for that plain old Rose Lilling, I'm going to scream."

"Rose Stone now," Emma corrected. "Poor Haydn, it must've broken his heart when she married Calvin Stone."

"Just proves my point, ladies," Margaret said, pointing the flower at the girls. "See what love does?"

"Well, maybe some day he'll fall in love again, and it won't end badly," Emma said.

"Are you volunteering to help him find a storybook ending?" one of the girls asked.

"That is my brother you're talking about, you

harlots," Margaret said, tossing the flower at Emma.

"Harlots?" Emma said. "We're not the ones refusing to marry." Emma picked up the flower and put it in her hair.

"Why don't you find someone else to rope into matrimony?" Margaret said.

"Well, then, how about Haydn's friend Edward Billingsley?" Emma said. "Isn't he the most handsome man you ever saw?"

"Oh, I don't know," Margaret said. "Peter Martin isn't exactly awful to look at."

The girls looked toward the solarium where Haydn, Edward and Peter talked animatedly with several friends.

Haydn and his friends Peter, Edward and Will were discussing the trips they'd taken to Europe the previous year and the colleges they planned to attend in the fall on the East Coast. Peter noticed that a gaggle of young women by the bay window were staring at them and giggling. He smiled back and inclined his head in greeting to them, then turned his attention back to the discussion at hand. Edward asked Haydn when he would start university classes and where.

"I'll work at the bank through the summer then start classes at University of Virginia in the fall," Haydn answered.

"Excellent!" Edward said. "I'll be starting there in

the fall myself. What are you going to study?"

"My father wants me to pursue a law degree," Haydn responded.

"Really? I never pictured you as a lawyer." Edward said.

Haydn shrugged.

"I never pictured him graduating grammar school, but somehow he came through," said Will. Haydn and Will had been best friends for as long as Haydn could remember. His favorite thing about Will was his sense of humor, which Will had developed to protect himself against those who teased him about his red hair, freckles and chubby frame.

Out of the corner of his eye, Haydn saw a couple with their arms entwined smiling at each other. His breath caught.

The woman looked in his direction. When she saw him, her smiled slipped. Then she returned her gaze to her companion, pretending she hadn't seen Haydn.

Peter, Edward and Will exchanged glances.

"He's hopeless you know," said Will.

"What?" Haydn asked, still staring at the couple.

"Calvin Stone—he's hopeless." Will snapped his fingers at Haydn, and Haydn's head twitched around. He looked at his friends, and his cheeks turned red. "The only reason he was around to steal Rose's heart was because his own father saw no point in sending him abroad for a year," Will continued. "He didn't even go east for college. He started classes at Baylor University in Waco in the fall, and according to my mother, he was home constantly. He ended up dropping out of school so he could stay here and marry Rose, and now he's working for his father in some position where he can't harm the business. He's never going to amount to anything on his own."

"I work for my father in a position where I can't do much harm," Haydn said.

"Nonsense," Willard said, waving his hand. "You're just marking time until you go to college. You'll be making your own fortune before you know it."

"No," Haydn said, looking back at the couple. "I'm marking time until I go off to college then come back to work for my father, who will decide how much of a fortune to give me. And someday, I'll work for my brother instead of my father. At least Calvin is in line to take over his father's company. No wonder Rose picked him over me."

"I'm not listening to this 'poor me' routine, Hy," Will said. "Who says you have to come back here and work for your father? Maybe you'll stay in Virginia and become a gentleman farmer, or go off to Washington and become a famous legislator. Or you'll come back here and invent beer that gets you just the right amount of drunk and no more."

"Oh yes, invent that!" said Peter.

"You just wait," Will put his hand on Haydn's shoulder. "Rose will regret breaking off your engagement, and you'll be glad she did. You'll have yourself a beautiful wife and ten sons, and Rose will be stuck with that hopeless twit. They'll probably have to settle for a herd of cats instead of children. Mark my words."

Haydn smiled despite himself at the image of Rose trying to corral an army of cats out of the house.

"I like cats," he said to Will.

"You're going to give me an attack," Will said and threw his arms up. "Okay, she'll be stuck with a house full of…little Calvins."

"Dear heaven," Haydn raised the back of his hand to his mouth in mock horror.

"Precisely!" Will said.

"If that's all settled, Billingsley and I are going to the buffet table," Peter said. "Anyone interested in food?"

"Just try and stop me," Will said and turned on his heel.

"Haydn?" Peter asked.

"I'll save our spot here," Haydn said. "You go ahead."

Haydn watched his friends make their way to the buffet then looked toward the east wall of the room where his brother and a group of friends were laughing around an ornate fireplace. He thought it must be nice to be so carefree about the future. George had good looks, an easy manner, plenty of friends, a secure career path— he had it all, except for a wife. But he was sure George would work that small detail out.

George had been engaged last year to Beatrice Wells, but the betrothal broke up before the family could have a formal engagement party. George wouldn't say why. But rather than being uncomfortable around one another, like Haydn and Rose, George and Beatrice were still friendly. It seemed to Haydn that it was only a matter of time before the pair reconciled and married. Bad things just didn't happen to George.

Everything came so easily for his brother, and Haydn always felt like he was swimming up from the bottom of the ocean, pushing against the pressure of the water, moving too slowly, the surface just out of reach. Haydn didn't so much feel envy as bafflement. How could they be so different?

A young woman hit George's shoulder with a fan.

"George!" she shouted and blushed. Her husband put his arm around her.

"Now, aren't you glad you're married to me and not that scoundrel, Daisy?" the man laughed, and George lifted his glass in salute.

"George wouldn't dream of getting married," said Beatrice.

"That's because I could never do any fine Galveston woman justice, Beatrice," George said and bowed to her.

"Was I really once charmed by that?" Beatrice asked, looking down at the top of his head.

"You wound me," George said, straightening up and trying to don a pained expression. "I think I'd better get another drink to dull the pain."

"And I think I'd like a bite to eat," Daisy said.

"May I escort you to the buffet table?" George asked, extending an arm to her.

"Thank you," Daisy said, taking George's arm.

They walked across the room to the west wall, where the refreshment table featured a large silver punch bowl filled with fruit punch. The punch bowl was flanked by floral arrangements and surrounded by platters of bon-bons, shrimp, oyster pâté, quail on toast, fruit, nuts and dainty sandwiches.

"Everything looks wonderful," Daisy said.

"The Martins serve only the best," Mildred said, approaching Daisy. "I don't believe we've met," she said, extending her hand. "My name is Mildred Winters."

"I'm Daisy Longfellow." Daisy shook her hand.

"Well, aren't you lovely?" Mildred said and looked at George.

"Oh, thank you," Daisy said, color rising in her cheeks.

"Daisy is Harold Longfellow's new bride, mother,"

George said. "Don't get any ideas."

"Don't be silly," Mildred said. "Of course I know all about Harold's marriage."

George looked at Mildred and raised an eyebrow. Mildred may have known that Harold Longfellow had married, but he was quite sure Mildred had no idea who Daisy was until this moment.

"Daisy, your Mr. Longfellow is a fine young man," Mildred said. "He's a BOI, you know."

"That stands for 'Born On the Island,'" George told Daisy. "I'll bet you didn't know that being born on this spit of sand granted you extra special status."

Daisy smiled uncertainly and looked from George to Mildred. Mildred's lips were pursed, and Daisy gripped a napkin.

"Mother, Daisy isn't interested in self-important titles," George said, shooing Mildred away with his hand. "She's interested in food. Leave her alone, and let her get a plate."

"Now, you're just being rude," Mildred said.

"There you are," said Harold, putting his arm around his wife's waist. "And how are you, Mrs. Winters?"

"Wonderful, Mr. Longfellow," Mildred said. "I was just talking to your lovely new wife about the beautiful table Mrs. Martin has provided for us."

"Mrs. Martin certainly knows how to entertain," Harold said. "Darling, I think Beatrice wanted to ask you something about your dress."

"Oh, I'll go see what she wanted," Daisy said and gave her husband a grateful look.

The couple bid Mildred a fine evening and headed back to the fireplace. George took an olive from a bowl and said to Mildred, "Good job, Mother. You ran her off without so much as a shrimp."

"I ran her off?" Mildred's eyes widened. "You couldn't have made her more uncomfortable if you'd tried."

"Oh, I'm sure I could have if I'd tried," he said, popping the olive into his mouth. "I'd love to talk about this more, but I need a drink." He walked off, leaving his mother angry but unable to respond without yelling after him and making a scene.

When he rejoined the group by the fireplace, one of the young men was asking Daisy, "Everything all right?"

"Yes, thank you," Daisy said.

"Watch it there," Harold said, mock glaring at the young man and tightening his arm around his wife. "She's mine now. If there are dragons to slay, I'll slay them. Brothers are only good for picking up the pieces after the dragon has won."

The young man laughed.

"Lloyd, I will always want you to protect me," Daisy said. "And Harold, you shouldn't compare Mrs. Winters to a dragon."

"No, he's got it about right," Beatrice said. "Dragons, George's mother—same thing. I don't know what went on over there, but don't let her run you back to Kansas just yet. You either, Lloyd. Your sister may need you if Harold goes to battle with that one."

George mimed the action of a dragon pouncing on Beatrice's shoulder, and she flicked him with her thumb and middle finger on the top of the head.

"Careful," George said, rubbing the spot where she'd flicked him. "You'll make me spill my drink."

"We would never intentionally offend Mrs. Winters," Daisy said to George, her brow knitted.

"I'm only teasing," Beatrice said and patted her hand. "There's nothing for you to worry about. You're new to town, so I probably shouldn't joke like that until you have a chance to get to know people. I just think Mildred Winters spends too much time noticing some things and not enough time noticing others. Let's talk about something more pleasant. Lloyd, how long will we have your company here in Galveston?"

"Well, actually, I'm thinking of staying."

Murmurs of "Wonderful!" and "Grand news!" passed through the group. George thought Beatrice seemed to particularly light up at this news.

"I was only supposed to bring Daisy down here to be married, but I think Galveston could be a wonderful place for a young man starting out in business. I've been thoroughly impressed with everything I've seen since I came." He looked at Beatrice.

"That's wonderful!" Daisy said and threw her arms around her brother's neck.

"Well, if you're going to stay, we'll have to make sure you're properly introduced to everyone," Beatrice said, taking Lloyd's arm. "Who haven't you met here tonight?"

George felt a pang in his stomach and drained his drink.

"Lots of people, but I think I've met most of the people who look our age," Lloyd said. "Harold said Mrs. Martin had a daughter our age, but I don't believe I've met her yet. Which one is she?"

"Gertrude married Adam Patterson a couple of years ago, and they don't socialize much," Beatrice explained.

Beatrice and George exchanged a look. Lloyd waited a beat to see if more explanation would be forthcoming. When it was not, he spoke up to fill the gap in conversation.

"Well, then, I suppose I've met everyone. This is a lovely party."

"This is nothing," George said, rattling the ice in his empty glass. His voice had a slight edge. "The old Mardi Gras celebrations would put this to shame."

"Well, I don't know if I'd say this one would be a shame," Beatrice said.

"I'm just saying the old days were more…theatrical,"

George said, looking hard at Beatrice and holding her eyes. He clenched his empty glass, and uncomfortable silence fell over the group.

After a few moments, Daisy spoke up, "I can't imagine anything more magical than this." George looked at her and his expression softened.

"In the old days, we used to have citywide Mardi Gras carnivals," George said. "When I was a kid, there were day and night street parades and masquerade balls with everyone in elaborate costumes. My mother told me they had hundreds of caged canaries as decoration at one of the balls."

"And there was a different theme every year," Beatrice added. "George, wasn't your mother crowned Queen one year?"

"I could call her over, and she'll tell you all about it," George said, looking at Beatrice and raising an eyebrow.

"Oh, would you?" Beatrice said. George noticed that she'd dropped Lloyd's arm, and he eased his grip on his glass.

"People sent out thousands of invitations all over the state," George said. "The governor even came one year."

"It sounds like such fun," Daisy said, her blue eyes wide. "Why don't they have all that anymore?"

"The parades got too expensive," George said. "So they started having private balls, and things just kind of fizzled."

"It sounds wonderful," said Daisy.

"It was," said Harold. "But we'll just have to make new memories, won't we? Come dance with me."

George watched them head to the portion of the room set aside for dancing. They were soon joined by several other couples.

"Would you like to dance?" George asked Beatrice. She hesitated a moment, glancing at Lloyd, then looked back at George.

"I'd love to," she said, giving him her hand.

CHAPTER 3

FEBRUARY 28, 1900

Rina Schmidt looked around the living room in Barton Mills' house. The room was not very large, but it was filled to capacity with neighborhood friends. She saw Barton turn a bottle of beer upside down, watch the drops dribble into a glass, then he announced, "I'm afraid we're empty, friends. Fat Tuesday is over!"

Rina laughed as people around the room pretended to mourn the passing of Fat Tuesday. They put their hats over their hearts and gave toasts with empty glasses. "Until we meet again, old friend." "'Tis truly sad to see you go, Fat One. Don't go losing any weight before we see you again next year." "It seems as though we hardly get started, and it's already gone."

Barton's party was always a hit in the neighborhood since he provided such a great spread of food, thanks to his job at Klaussen's Dry Goods. Barton didn't advertise the fact, but Mr. Klaussen gave him a discount on items at the store, which helped a great deal. Providing for a family on a deliveryman's salary could be a challenge.

As the toasts continued, Rina pulled a shawl across her shoulders and found her friend Melanie. "I'm heading home now."

"Are you sure? I'm sure people will stay until the food is gone."

"Absolutely. I have to work tomorrow. I can't stay up all night."

Katarina Schmidt, or Rina to her friends, was small and pretty with hazel eyes and curly, light brown hair that fell past her shoulders when she didn't wear it swept up. She and Melanie had been best friends since grade school, and they almost always attended parties together, though now that Melanie was engaged, Rina sometimes felt like a third wheel.

"Wait just a second, and I'll get my coat," Melanie said.

"Don't be silly," Rina patted Melanie's arm. "John isn't ready to go yet, and you don't want him thinking his fiancée is a wet blanket, do you?"

Melanie glanced at her newly betrothed, John, talking animatedly with another man. "You really don't mind walking by yourself?"

"Not a bit," Rina said. "I'll talk to you tomorrow."

A few moments later, Rina was walking in the glow

of the moon, which was high and full. She pulled her wrap around her and felt invigorated and relaxed at the same time. As she got closer to the beach, a cold breeze lifted her hair and washed salt air across her face.

She liked to come to the beach by herself, particular when she knew no one else would be there, and sit on the dunes, watching the surf. She made her way to a dune with grass growing on the top like a mat and was about to sit down when she saw something on the beach.

* * *

Around 1:00 a.m., the Martins' guests began to disperse. George left the party with a few male companions to find other opportunities to revel near Post Office Street.

"Hy, shall we head to Post Office, too?' Will asked.

"I don't think so," Haydn said. "I'm tired, and I'm feeling the drink I've had tonight."

Will shrugged. "Well, don't mope too much. It'll make your hangover worse," he said and headed out the door with Billingsley and Peter.

The truth was Haydn had hardly imbibed at all. He had nursed just two drinks all night. He had expected that seeing Rose with Calvin Stone would deliver a stab of pain. It had the other times he'd seen the pair around town. But for some reason, when he saw them tonight, the stab didn't come. He'd felt the familiar catch of breath when he first spotted Rose, and the encounter was uncomfortable, but the pain in his gut didn't come this time. He was unsure how to feel about that.

Most of his friends would have used the experience as an excuse to drink themselves into blackness, but Haydn knew that for him, drinking only intensified whatever he was feeling, and the last thing he wanted to do was amplify what he felt. At the moment, he couldn't quite describe what he felt, but whatever it was, it was awkward and didn't need intensifying.

So, he had nursed his drinks, smiled amiably at his friends' jokes and waited for the evening to end. Relieved that it was now over, he stepped onto the sidewalk outside the Martin home, heard his friends disappear noisily down the street and wondered where to go next. He didn't want to go home, where his mother might still be awake, ready to share her views about Rose—again. And he didn't want to go anyplace where he might be expected to continue celebrating, which eliminated most inhabited parts of the island. So, he walked to the beach.

The beach was cold and dark when he arrived, lending the perfect backdrop for his wandering thoughts. The clouds passed by overhead, periodically parting so the moon could cast a wide, bright light on the sand and surf. The rhythmic sound of the waves, with the occasional small crash of water tumbling over itself, mirrored his emotions. He felt a constant restlessness lately, and he was unsure what caused it.

Was it the anticipation of leaving for college? Was it the fear of doing so? He didn't want to be a lawyer, so was it the fear of telling his father so? Or the fear of not telling him? Was it the pain of his broken engagement with Rose? No, that wasn't it. He was sure of that now.

He picked up a shell and skipped it into the receding surf and thought about Rose. As painful as the breakup had been, and as uncomfortable as he felt when he saw her now, he wasn't even sure he particularly wanted her anymore. At the party, he felt like he should say something when Will had tried to make him feel better about seeing her. But he wasn't sure he could explain what he felt, so he just let Will reassure him that the broken engagement was all for the best. Someday, when he could say something coherent about the whole affair, he'd tell Will that he agreed.

He shook his head to dispel the thoughts of Rose and picked up another shell. Tossing it into the water, he decided he would concentrate instead on his plans to leave Galveston. While he didn't feel a particular pull toward Virginia, he did feel the need to get away from Galveston. As unclear as he was about his feelings for Rose, that's how sure he was of his feelings about leaving Galveston. It was time to go. Or at least it would be in seven months. He just had to bide his time until the fall semester.

As he walked on the sand in the dark, by the light of the full moon, he thought about college and how he might be able to sidestep his father's plans for him.

He could go to the University of Virginia as planned, but instead of taking classes to earn a law degree, he could work toward the English literature degree he wanted instead. He felt certain his father would barely take notice of what he was doing until he was far enough along in his degree to make changing to law an unreasonable proposition. By then, Haydn hoped that he would have a convincing argument as to the merits of his becoming an English professor instead of a lawyer for the family business.

He really wanted to just be a writer, but he knew that would never be acceptable to his parents. His grandmother Dorothea, who he'd always called Nana, had always loved to read his short stories and his poetry. When he was a child, they'd sit for hours on the sunny porch on the side of the house. Haydn would spin grand tales about the birds and bugs they'd see inhabiting the grounds, and Nana would ask leading questions.

"Where are they going, child? What's that one saying?"

After Nana died, he had tried a time or two to engage his mother in one of his daydreamy scenarios or to show her one of his short stories, but Mildred always said she didn't have time for such nonsense. He never even tried with his father. He'd never known his father to read anything but the newspaper. George had found one of his stories once and had teased him mercilessly about it, so he was careful now to keep his writing stowed carefully away in his room in a trunk.

He still went to the sun porch, though, when he wanted to be creative or sentimental. And when he felt particularly moved to share his creative thoughts with someone, he went to the stable where the carriage horses were kept and confided in them or Buddy. Dogs and horses were outstanding listeners.

Sometimes, he pretended that Nana was there with him on the porch or in the stable. He talked to her when he needed a sympathetic ear and tried to imagine what words of comfort she might have for him. Sometimes, as he thought of her possible response, he wondered if maybe they really were her words—if she was listening in heaven and putting the words in his head, talking to him in the way only she could.

In fact, he credited her with putting the idea in his head that perhaps he could convince his parents that teaching was worthwhile, and then he could still write in his spare time. Maybe he'd even like teaching.

Haydn's confidence in his ability to sway Joseph had taken a bit of a stumble at the party tonight. He'd overheard Joseph talking to Mr. Martin about one of

George's schoolmates, James Kingston. Joseph went on about the pathetic waste of James becoming a newspaper reporter.

"Newspapers? That's not working," Joseph had argued. "That's telling about other people working. His father must be mortified. Phillip Kingston offered that boy a golden opportunity with his shipping company, and that ungrateful upstart threw it away to become a gossip. That's all those reporters are - just a bunch of gossips. He's no better than the women who sit around here in their sewing circles like hens, clucking about who wore what to which tea. And what is Phillip supposed to do? James was his only son. Is he supposed to give the company to his daughter when he retires?"

That elicited a chuckle from Mr. Martin.

"He's going to have to leave the company that he and his father built from the ground up, through unions and storms and the War, to some hired hand. Kingston Shipping will no longer have a Kingston at the helm."

Mr. Martin shook his head and said simply, "Damn shame."

Joseph seemed to miss the irony that his own career and social status had started with him as beneficiary of that exact scenario.

When Haydn first heard the exchange, it disheartened him. He could just hear what Joseph would say when he told him what he wanted to do. *Good God,*

Haydn, do you seriously propose to make a living reading books and talking about something as pointless as literature? Could you possibly devise a bigger waste of your life?

But as he looked out over the ocean, rubbing a shell between his thumb and forefinger, he decided to view the exchange as insight into possible objections his father might raise. He'd have an entire year, more maybe, to come up with an answer to those objections.

He began to pace on the sand as his mind churned with possible arguments in his favor. Soon, he was speaking aloud, practicing his argument to his father.

"Father, you don't really need me at the bank," he reasoned to the empty night. "George is the one who will someday take over, not me. And while I concede the merits of having an in-house attorney, it isn't as if it's a necessity. Look at the business you've already built without one. Why, I'd probably just be in the way more than anything else." *That might do it, mightn't it? He tends to think of me as a bit in the way as it is.*

The more he presented his case out loud, the more animated he became. It was a long shot, but if Haydn played it right, it might work. And by the time it even became necessary to have the conversation, well, who knew how much more important George might be to the business by then?

If it worked, maybe he'd just stay in Virginia after he graduated. He doubted his family would argue to bring him home, particularly if he wasn't going to be part of the business and was going to be doing something as frivolous as teaching or writing.

The thought of the freedom of living in Virginia, away from his family, making his own decisions about his life, made Haydn reach his hands to the sky and laugh out loud. He was mid-guffaw when he noticed a young woman watching him, moving cautiously away from him.

"Oh, hello," he said pulling his hands down to his sides. He felt his face color and was glad it was too dark for her to see.

The woman froze at being spotted.

"I must look quite mad," Haydn said, forcing a chuckle and trying to sound nonchalant.

"I…I'm sorry," the woman stammered. "I didn't mean to…I should go." She began to back away, but kept her eye on Haydn. Haydn could see even in the moonlight that she was attractive.

"It's all right. Really it is," he said. "I was just practicing something." He took a step in her direction. "Really - I don't normally walk around talking to myself."

"I'm sure you don't," she said, backing up faster. "It's late, though. And cold. And I'm sure my friends are looking for me. Good night." She turned and scampered over the dune.

"Good night!" he yelled after her and watched her run from the beach until he could no longer see her.

CHAPTER 4

FEBRUARY 28, 1900

Ash Wednesday was cold and quiet. Galveston always awoke the day after Mardi Gras to an aching head and promises to be more pious next year. As the sun began to lighten the sky, evidence of a long night of celebration littered the streets, and city crews were beginning to clean up the aftermath.

Rina avoided the dirty streets and walked on the beach, feeling the sand shift under her lace-up boots. She would have to dodge the trash soon enough on her walk to work, and she preferred to start the day with a visit to the beach when she could manage it. She liked her job at Mrs. Heckmann's Dress Shoppe, but time on the beach was preferable to time anywhere else.

She listened to the gulls, smelled the faint odor of fish, and breathed in the cold, thick, salt air, pretending not to notice that the moisture-laden breeze made her coat feel as if it were made of lace.

The section of beach she walked on this morning was the same part of the shore she'd visited last night after Barton Mills' party. She thought about the man she had seen. She knew it was not proper for her to be out alone on the beach at night, and she realized how stupid she had been to think that there wouldn't be drunks out.

When she topped the dune last night, she saw the man talking to himself and gesturing to the heavens. When he began to laugh and become more animated, Rina tried to steal slowly away, but he had spotted her.

When he tried to speak to her, her heart started pounding. She could see that he was young and, if she was honest, handsome. He didn't sway or have the lax features of drunkenness or even slur his words now that she thought about it. Could it be he wasn't drunk? He must be unbalanced, then. She felt a little disappointed.

This morning, looking around the same spot of beach, the whole scene seemed like a hallucination.

She arrived at work, and Mrs. Heckmann was already bustling between the shop's front room reception and its back room work area.

"Rina, I thought you'd never get here," she said breathlessly. "Today will be very busy. We must make room in the back for all the dresses that will be coming in for cleaning and mending."

Rina remembered this routine from New Year's Day. The week before a night of parties and balls was a blur of activity, with Rina, Mrs. Heckmann, and Rina's co-worker Mrs. Werner working like ants to finish all their customers' party dresses. Then the week after the parties was the same bustle of activity, cleaning and mending those same dresses. Rina did not mind, though. It made the day go by quickly when they were busy.

"I'll start on that right away, Mrs. Heckmann." She hung up her coat and went to the back room, dodging the sewing tables and dress forms hung with unfinished dresses and started clearing the room for the morning's arrivals.

Mrs. Werner had not arrived yet. Rina knew she would arrive soon, but Rina would likely have the room organized and ready for the day's work by the time she arrived, murmuring, "My dear, how efficient you are."

* * *

Haydn entered the dining room to find his family, except for Margaret, already at the table. Everyone but his mother was eating.

"Long night, little brother?" George sounded cheerful but his red-rimmed eyes betrayed that he could have used a few more hours of sleep himself.

"Not as long as yours."

George saluted Haydn with a glass of tomato juice, and Haydn seated himself.

"Would you like orange juice, Mr. Haydn, or tomato juice like Mr. George?" Jefferson asked.

Haydn eyed the tomato juice. George winked at him. "It'll cure what ails you."

"Thank you, Jefferson. I'll have plain orange juice," Haydn said, emphasizing the word "plain."

"George, I saw you dancing last night with Beatrice," Mildred said.

"Did you?" George raised eyebrows. "And I thought we were being so secretive, doing it right there on the dance floor with everyone else."

"Don't be smart," Mildred said. "I'm just saying that it seemed you two were getting on awfully well."

"We always get on awfully well."

"Well, not always, or you would still be engaged," Mildred said.

George looked down at his plate, and Haydn could see a muscle in his jaw tensing.

"Have you reconsidered your engagement to her?" Mildred pressed.

"It wasn't for me to reconsider, Mother," George said evenly.

"I think Beatrice is nice," Haydn said.

"That's because she is," George said. "She has lots of wonderful qualities. We all agree, then? Beatrice is perfect." He slammed his glass down.

"I'm sorry. I wasn't trying to—" Haydn started, but was cut off by Mildred.

"I just think it's strange how you two go on," Mildred said. "It was an absolute scandal when you broke off your engagement. You two seemed so suited to one another, perfectly matched socially. But instead of wedding, you part ways for no reason. Except you don't part ways. You alternately appear to be still courting or nothing more than acquaintances, depending on the day. I can't understand it."

"I think 'absolute scandal' is overstating it a bit," George said. He wiped his mouth with a napkin and threw it on the table.

"That's enough gossip," Joseph announced, folding his paper. "If I listen to much more of this, I'll have to take up knitting and start wearing dresses. Boys, let's go."

"You know, Father, some businesses actually give their employees a holiday today," George said as he got to his feet.

"Is there a newspaper today?" Joseph asked.

"Yes, sir," George rolled his eyes.

"Then Galveston is doing business, and Galveston Fidelity is open." Joseph folded the newspaper and stuffed it under his arm. He turned to leave the room.

"There's a paper on Sunday, and we're closed then," George said to Joseph's back.

"Well, then you've got it better than some people, don't you?" Joseph said as the dining room door closed behind him.

Haydn rose from the table, and he and George went to the foyer. They put on their coats, and Joseph opened the front door.

"Haydn, wait," Mildred called after them. "I want you to take Margaret's dress to Mrs. Heckmann's to be cleaned."

Haydn scrunched his face. "Why isn't Jefferson doing that?" He didn't want to incur his mother's wrath by complaining and quickly said, "I'll be late to work." He glanced at his father, hoping Joseph would step in on his behalf.

"I have things I need Jefferson to do at the house today, and I don't want him traipsing all over town," Mildred said. "Don't question me. Just do what I ask."

"See you in a bit, errand boy," George tousled Haydn's hair, and he and Joseph left.

Five minutes later, Haydn left the house with Margaret's dress draped over his arm. He hoped that his friends were either already at work or sleeping late after the long night so they wouldn't see him running domestic errands for his little sister.

Overflow

Margaret sat upstairs at her vanity. She stared into the mirror and counted the number of times she pulled a silver paddle brush through her long, blonde hair. She brushed it exactly 100 strokes every morning.

Sometimes she became mesmerized watching the moving reflection of her monogram on the back of the brush: a large W in the center, with an M to the left, and an A to the right. The A bothered her because it was a reminder of her middle name, Agnes. Margaret thought it a hideous name and had said so to her mother, who shared it as a middle name.

The M and W pleased her, though. In the mirror, the positions of the letters were reversed, but they looked the same. If you saw the scene without the benefit of the mirror frame, she thought, it would be difficult to tell which image was an illusion and which was the real Margaret.

Sallie knocked twice and, without waiting for an answer from Margaret, entered the room carrying a clean towel. She set the towel on the bed, took a long-sleeved green dress with a velvet collar from the closet and placed it next to the towel.

"Ma'am said for you to wear this one today, Miss," Sallie said.

Margaret kept counting.

Sallie crossed to the fireplace. In the mirror's reflection, Margaret saw her stoke the fire into an active blaze and pretend to push the logs around with the poker for a few moments as the fire warmed her.

Then she watched Sallie walk to the bathroom adjoining Margaret's bedroom. Sallie had run bath water a half hour earlier into Margaret's claw foot tub, but Margaret hadn't managed to get into the bath before the water had gotten cold. She now heard the water draining. After enough had drained out, Sallie would turn on the "hot" spigot and refill the tub.

Margaret knew that while she waited for the tub to refill, Sallie would quietly inspect the room's contents. It was an invasion of privacy, but Margaret pretended not to know what the girl was doing. Sallie never took anything, and Margaret knew she must wonder what it would be like to bathe in lilac scented water and to wear a silk robe.

She wished she could tell Sallie that silk shackles were shackles nonetheless, but she didn't think the girl would appreciate the sentiment. While Margaret might wish she were free to pursue her passions to paint and travel and explore the world, she knew that Sallie would only see her as ungrateful for all that she had.

To Sallie, a life of card parties and social calls might sound perfectly lovely. To Margaret, it sounded inane. It was possible that Sallie had no interest in ever leaving this tiny little island in the Gulf of Mexico, but Margaret wanted to see Paris, Rome, Greece, where art lived and breathed.

And while she didn't despise the idea of men—she quite liked some of them—she didn't much care for what a husband meant. Husband meant master, and she already had one of those in her mother. She didn't want some man telling her where she could go, how she could spend her money, what art she could look at, what art she could create. No, better to be alone than to be controlled.

Margaret's brush caught a tangle, and when she tugged out the knot, she thought she had given herself a bald patch. After reassuring herself that her hair was still intact, she resumed brushing but eased up on the force she was using on the brush. Sallie exited the bathroom and crossed the room without saying a word.

When Margaret heard Sallie's footsteps retreat down the hall, she set down her brush. She retrieved from the closet a simple, cotton dress and a paint-stained smock and tossed them on top of the green dress. She picked up the towel from the bed and entered the bathroom.

She pinned up her hair and slipped off her nightgown then lowered herself into the warm water.

* * *

"Margaret will have one egg and toast with marmalade, Jefferson," Mildred Winters said as Jefferson pushed through the door to the dining room with a silver coffee service tray. "She'll be down any moment, and I want to be served as soon as she's seated."

She didn't need to tell Jefferson her own order because she always had the same breakfast: one poached egg and one slice of ham, not touching.

"Yes, ma'am," Jefferson said, setting the tray on a large mahogany sideboard to the right of the door leading from the kitchen. He took the coffeepot to the table, waited for Mrs. Winters to nod that she was ready for him to pour, then he carefully filled her cup. He stepped back to the sideboard and exchanged the coffeepot for the sugar and cream containers and flavored her coffee to her liking, then returned to the kitchen.

She tried not to show her aggravation as the minutes ticked by without Margaret's appearance at the table. She didn't want the servants to see that Margaret could get the better of her. But a half an hour later, when Margaret entered the dining room, she stiffened.

"What are you wearing?" she demanded, as Jefferson pushed into the room.

"I'll have toast with marmalade and a piece of ham, Jefferson," Margaret said.

"I told Sallie to lay out your green dress," Mildred said. "We're going to call on Mrs. Exbridge this afternoon."

"Oh, and I'll have orange juice, too," Margaret called

after Jefferson as he disappeared into the kitchen.

"Did you hear me?" Mildred slapped a spoon on the table.

Margaret pretended to pick at a speck on her smock.

"So defiant," Mildred shook her head. "Fine, then. You may play with your paints this morning, but you will be ready to call on Mrs. Exbridge at one o'clock. And there will not be one drop of paint on you or so much as a hint of turpentine smell. Do you hear me?"

Mildred spread her napkin across her lap. She didn't understand why Margaret had to fight her on everything. She was doing her best to make Margaret a respected member of Galveston society, despite the girl's seeming desire to ruin her own future with her willfulness. Several of Mildred's contemporaries had commented that Margaret certainly seemed to be high-spirited, which Mildred knew was not a compliment. If she didn't find a husband for Margaret soon, the girl was likely to end up a spinster, and Mildred would surely be a laughing stock.

Jefferson returned to the room and placed a glass of orange juice and a plate of eggs and toast in front of Margaret. Mildred was pleased to see that he had not given Margaret toast and ham as her daughter had asked, but was instead following the instructions she had issued.

"Thank you, Jefferson. This is lovely," she said and gave Mildred a sharp look.

"I asked you a question," Mildred said. "Are we clear

about this afternoon?"

Margaret took a long drink of orange juice, set her glass on the table, then met Mildred's eyes.

"I'm sorry, Mother. Did you say something?"

CHAPTER 5

FEBRUARY 28, 1900

This is just insulting, Haydn thought as he walked sullenly to the seamstress shop. *She'd never ask George to do some sort of domestic errand. And I'm a professional in the family business now, just like he is! Or at least I will be. Unless, of course, I decide not to come back to Galveston. Deliver me from this island! And thank God Will can't see this.*

The bell above the doorway of the seamstress shop announced Haydn's arrival. Mrs. Heckmann entered the front room.

"Good morning, sir, how may I help you?"

"My name is Haydn Winters. I believe my mother called this morning to tell you I'd be bringing my sister Margaret's dress in." He lifted the dress to show her.

"Yes. It needs to be cleaned and a hem mended, correct?" she said, taking the dress from him and inspecting the bottom rim of the dress.

"You'll have to talk to my mother about that. I'm just delivering it."

"I see," she said and gave him a practiced smile. "Well, we'll take care of this as if it belonged to a queen, Mr. Winters." She turned away, opened the door leading to the back work area and hung the dress on a bar mounted just inside the door. Through the open door, Haydn saw a young woman working in the back room. His eyes fixed on her and his mouth dropped open. The door shut, and the girl was gone.

Haydn's mind raced. He was sure the girl behind the door was the girl from the beach last night. Embarrassment alone would have been enough to burn the girl's face into his brain, but add her beauty to the mix, and he couldn't possibly forget her. He felt a flutter in his stomach.

"Anything else, Mr. Winters?" Mrs. Heckmann asked. Haydn was staring at the closed door.

"No, no, thank you for your help," he said, dragging his eyes to meet the shop owner's. He opened the front door to leave. The bell on top of the shop's door tinkled, and Haydn looked back once more in case he might be afforded one more glance into the back room, but the older woman stood motionless at the desk watching him, and the door remained closed.

* * *

The morning went by quickly for George. He worked on the bank's real estate accounts, logging in rents collected and balancing the books. Galveston Fidelity held the mortgages on several properties on the island, and one of his responsibilities was to maintain the paperwork and manage collections for all of the bank's real estate holdings, as well as manage the rental income from some of Joseph's privately owned residential rental properties.

He barely noticed when Haydn arrived at the bank, but he did notice as the day wore on that Haydn seemed distracted and not particularly productive. He saw his father give Haydn several stern glances when his younger brother gazed absentmindedly out the bank's windows and leaned lazily on the counter. Each time, when Haydn would finally realize that Joseph was staring at him, he would straighten up and begin to tidy deposit slips near his window or the bills in his drawer, before getting lost in his thoughts again.

George knew that Joseph thought Haydn was still just a boy, rather than a man. He had heard his father complain to his mother many times that Haydn seemed to live in his own thoughts, jotting down God knows what on scraps of paper and staring out into the trees.

He even heard Joseph tell Mildred one time that he was relieved he had George to hand the bank over to some day. He said it would be struggle enough to toughen Haydn to handle the legal affairs of the family's businesses. He couldn't imagine handing over the entire bank to him.

"Business is sometimes an unpleasant affair," he had told her. "It requires difficult decisions and cunning negotiation. To be successful, a man must be able to mask his emotions. He must be able to finesse people and situations. George can finesse anyone. But Haydn? I just don't see it, Mildred."

George had felt a twinge of resentment at the time, hearing his father plan out his life as if he had no vote in the matter. But when he realized that he didn't really know what else he would do if he didn't work at the bank, the resentment had faded into resignation. And he knew that Joseph was right about Haydn.

He looked at his younger brother leaning on the counter and shook his head. He loved Haydn and knew he had wonderful qualities, but he wasn't sure Haydn would ever be suited to the demands of a business attorney. No, Haydn was more like their grandfather, Joseph's father, Nathan.

Haydn resembled his grandfather physically. His frame was a mirror image of Nathan's. His hands were not callused, as Nathan's had been, but the way he moved his hands, and the way he cocked his head when he was thinking hard…sometimes it was as if Nathan was in the room. But mostly, it was in Haydn's personality that George saw his grandfather. And he knew his father saw it, too.

"Good God, it's like dealing with Father all over again!" Joseph had said in a moment of exasperation to his mother, Dorothea, when Haydn was about five.

"Isn't it wonderful?" she had said, beaming, and Joseph had walked away frustrated. George hadn't understood then, being a child himself, and he asked his father later what he had meant about Haydn.

"Your grandfather was a good man, but he always had trouble understanding what was important," Joseph explained to him. "I don't know that I ever saw him read *The Daily News* front to back, yet he would spend hours in the pages of a novel. What's the use of that?"

George hadn't been sure how to answer, so he just stayed quiet.

"If my father had applied himself to knowing important people in town and staying current on matters of industry and finance," Joseph had continued, "he might have created more opportunities for himself, and thus, the rest of us—his family. But instead, he just wasted his hours away from work. Your brother is cut from the same cloth."

"Grandfather always seemed happy," George said softly.

"Oh, I'll give him that," Joseph conceded. "He could certainly entertain himself, and I suppose when I was a child, it entertained me, too. Did I ever tell you about the lady with the parasol?"

"No," George said.

"Well, he came home from work one day, and he asked me, 'Joseph, do you know who I saw on the street today?' I asked him who. 'I saw a grand lady in a pink dress with a pink parasol, and a man following her with so many boxes he couldn't see over them.'

"I asked him what was in the boxes. 'Why, it could've been anything!' he said. Then he asked me, 'What do you think was in them?' as if I could possibly know. When I couldn't think of an answer, he began to speculate. 'I think it was all new parasols, one in every color to match all of her dresses.'"

"I was incredulous. I asked him if anyone would really have so many parasols, and he said, 'Oh, a grand lady is likely to own anything, Joseph. She might even have had horseshoes in all those boxes.' Horseshoes! Well, then I knew he was just being ridiculous, so I asked him what a grand lady would possibly want with horseshoes, and you know what he said?"

"What?" George's eyes were wide.

"He said, 'Why, to have them painted pink so that

her carriage steeds' shoes would match her dress and parasol!'"

George keeled backward with laughter.

"For the longest time, I checked the horseshoes of passing carriages, looking for colored shoes, but I never saw any," Joseph admitted. "It was all nonsense. When I got older and refused to play such silly games, your grandmother started playing along. I told her she shouldn't encourage him, but she just said I should try to have more fun." Joseph harumphed into his mustache at the memory.

George thought his grandmother had a point, but he kept the thought to himself.

"I told Father he should be speculating on the cotton exchange," Joseph went on, "not on what's in some stranger's shopping parcels. I told him that wasting time on make believe was what had kept him in someone else's employ with little to show for a lifetime of labor."

"And he made matters worse by routinely coming home with stray dogs and cats to feed, even though we barely had enough food to eat ourselves. Does that sound like anyone else you know?"

George knew Haydn had been feeding some kittens in the alley and had tried to sneak one in the house. He didn't want to criticize his little brother, though, so he didn't respond. The kid just had a soft heart.

"Mother never complained, though," Joseph shook

his head. "She'd pet the creatures and find some old piece of cloth and put it on the porch for them to sleep on. She'd sit out there sometimes with them, letting them lie against her feet as she rubbed their fur. She was a wonderful woman with inexhaustible patience.

"I know that people say that's a virtue, George, but it's not always an estimable quality," Joseph shook a finger at George. "My father would have been served by my mother showing him less tolerance and more backbone. And I won't make that same mistake with Haydn."

"Father, were you poor?" George asked, wide-eyed.

"Well, we didn't live on an alley, and we weren't hungry, if that's what you mean," Joseph said, his cheeks coloring a little. "But we could have been more comfortable if your grandmother had been more insistent that your grandfather provide better for us.

"Instead of renting whatever small, wood-frame house had the best rent, we could have owned a home. And there was always food on the table, but it was usually the same food. Just about every morning of my childhood, we ate biscuits and coffee," Joseph rolled his eyes.

"No orange juice?" George asked. Orange juice was his favorite drink, and he couldn't imagine having to drink coffee instead.

"No orange juice," Joseph said. "And most nights,

we ate a dish of potatoes and onions. Potatoes and onions every night."

"We never have potatoes and onions," George said.

"You're damn right we don't!" Joseph said.

George wondered if he'd said something wrong. He hoped not. He wanted Joseph to go on. He'd never had this kind of one-on-one conversation with his father.

"And every night," Joseph picked back up, "as if the meal itself weren't detestable enough, my father would tell her it was delicious, then help clear the table, clean the dishes and put them away. I knew from my friends that other fathers didn't do such chores. Cooking and cleaning is woman's work, and if the other boys knew my father performed such feminine tasks, I would have been teased mercilessly. So, I never told a soul."

George felt tears creeping into his eyes with the pride of being his father's confidante. But he didn't want Joseph to think he was soft, so he quickly asked a question as he surreptitiously wiped away the moisture. "What did grandfather do for a living?"

Joseph paused, then answered, "He was a house mover."

George knew that some people on the island owned their houses, but not the land upon which they stood. He frequently watched with rapt attention as big trucks slowly crept through the streets, moving houses from one location to another. He was fascinated by the idea that his grandfather had been one of the men making this feat possible.

George had watched the crews work, and now he imagined his grandfather leading such a move, telling his men where to put the support beams under the house and calling out when everything was in position to start moving the structure. He could see the faces of the anxious homeowners as their homes inched through the streets to their new resting places. He pictured Nathan standing back, hands on his hips, as his crew placed a house on its new lot and the homeowners let out their breaths. It was a circus act, and his grandfather was the grand master.

George swelled with pride. But when he looked at his father, Joseph didn't seem to share that feeling. Joseph looked away and then said, "He was a laborer. He spent his life moving other people's homes and never owned one himself."

George had never thought about their house before—who built it or how they came to live in it. It's just where he had always lived.

"Do we own this house?" he asked, worried that it might be the wrong question but wanting to know.

"Of course," Joseph said, looking at him with surprise. Then he had patted George on the back and left.

Feeling nostalgic at the memory, George looked over at Joseph. But Joseph did not look nostalgic. He was looking at Haydn, who had his head cocked to the side, distracted again.

Joseph snatched up some papers from his desk and said, "I have to make some business calls." He grabbed his overcoat and banged open the bank's front door.

George jumped up and ran to get his coat, leaving his papers splayed across his desk.

"Did you want me to come with you?" he called out to Joseph. Receiving no answer, he looked to Haydn and Stefan, as if to inquire if he'd missed Joseph asking him to come. Haydn shrugged, and George ran out the door.

Haydn went over to George's desk to straighten the papers. If Joseph came back and saw the desk a mess, he would be angry.

Haydn looked at the papers as he straightened them and sighed. *What a mess,* he thought. The papers showed rents collected in some of the apartment buildings that Joseph owned, and George had clearly written, erased and rewritten the numbers several times. It wasn't like George to be so sloppy with his recordkeeping, and he knew Joseph would not approve. *I'd hate to be George if Father ever looks at these,* he thought.

He put the papers in a folder and left them on George's desk.

When he returned to his place at the counter, Stefan asked him, "My boy, what occupies your mind this morning? You are millions of miles from this bank."

"Oh, it's nothing," Haydn answered. "I just had an interesting night."

"I'm sure you did! It must have been a wonderful party," Stefan said.

"Yes, it was a nice party." Haydn leaned on the counter.

"Nice? That does not sound like a word for a Mardi Gras party," Stefan said, raising an eyebrow.

"Well, the interesting part was later."

"Interesting. That's a better word. What happened after the party that was interesting?" Stefan asked.

"Well, don't get too excited," Haydn said. "It wasn't interesting in the way that things get interesting for George after a party, if that's what you're thinking.

"I didn't think anything," Stefan said, raising his palms.

"I didn't go gambling or to the brothels. I just went to the beach to think."

"And did you think?"

"Yes, I did. I thought a lot. But then there was this girl."

"A girl! Now we get to the interesting part," Stefan said and smiled.

"I barely even spoke to her," Haydn said. "But I think I made an impression."

Haydn recounted the events of the night before. He

had been stricken about his encounter on the beach at the time, but as he related the exchange now to Stefan, he laughed. If it had happened to Will instead of himself, he would've thought the whole scene hysterical.

"Here's the best part," he said, now warmed to his subject. "This morning, I had to deliver Margaret's dress to the dress shop by the Opera House, and Stefan, I'm almost positive I saw the girl working there."

"You don't say," Stefan said, now leaning on the counter as well.

"I know it sounds improbable," Haydn said, "but I really think it was her."

"Well, then," Stefan said and slapped a hand on the counter. "What do you make of such providence?"

"What is there to make of it?" Haydn asked, unsure what Stefan meant.

"Whatever you choose to, my boy." He took Haydn by the shoulders and added, "Providence is what you make of it."

Haydn smiled at the old man and said, "Then I'll think about what to make of it."

"Well, don't think too long. Even providence can get tired of waiting. It's Wednesday," Stefan said, changing course. "What did you bring me to read?"

"It's been a busy week, with Mardi Gras and everything," Haydn said. "So, I haven't really written anything, but I think I might feel a poem coming on."

"You haven't done a poem in a long time," Stefan said. "I look forward to reading a new one."

* * *

That evening after dinner, Haydn entered the parlor where his father sat reading the newspaper and his mother worked on an embroidery project. He seated himself in a chair and drummed his fingers on his thighs.

"What is that you're working on?" he asked Mildred.

She looked up at him in surprise.

"Since when are you interested in my embroidery?"

"I was just curious," he shrugged. "It's very colorful."

"It's a sampler for Gertrude Patterson's new baby," she said and resumed working thread through the cloth.

"She's having a baby?" Haydn asked.

"I should think it's about time she did," Mildred said. "She's been married to Adam Patterson for more than two years. She never entertains or even socializes. If she's going to lock herself inside that house that Mr. Martin bought them as a wedding gift, she may as well raise some children."

Haydn didn't respond. He knew why Gertrude didn't socialize, but it was clear his mother either didn't know or didn't care, so he left the subject alone.

"Did Mrs. Heckmann say when Margaret's dress

would be ready?" he asked, trying to appear casual.

Mildred looked up again and studied him. "What's gotten into you tonight, asking so many questions about household affairs? You are a strange young man, Haydn Winters."

"I just thought that since I'd dropped off the dress, you'd probably want me to pick it up for you, too. I just wanted to plan for the extra errand."

"I'll have Jefferson do it," Margaret said. "He'll have time tomorrow."

"I really don't mind," Haydn said. "You say it's tomorrow? It would be no problem at all. The dress shop is only a few blocks from the bank. Why don't I go pick it up at lunch and bring it home, and when I get here, Elinor can have some lunch ready for me?"

Mildred removed the small glasses she wore when she embroidered, and looked at him for several seconds. She then put the glasses back on and returned to her sampler.

"If you wish. Tell Elinor tomorrow morning what you shall have for lunch so she'll have it ready."

"Of course," Haydn said, excitedly rising from his chair. He caught himself and tried to appear relaxed. "I think I'll go find a book to read."

He walked casually out of the room and bounded up the stairs.

CHAPTER 6

MARCH 1, 1900

By Thursday, Galveston was operating at full speed again. The hangovers from Mardi Gras were forgotten, and the Galveston Fidelity Bank, like the rest of the city, had resumed its normal brisk pace.

Haydn and Stefan conducted business with customers almost without interruption, while Joseph met with a number of high-profile customers during the morning, discussing their financial plans for the year and Galveston Fidelity's role in them.

Haydn heard some of the men express concern about Houston's plan for a deep water port, wondering how much business that might take away from Galveston's port. But Joseph assured them that Houston was destined to be little more than a mosquito-laden swamp and would never approach the level of business transacted in Galveston.

George finished the paperwork on the real estate accounts that he'd had to leave on his desk the day before. Yesterday, when he had returned from his errand with Joseph to find the pages neatly waiting in a pile, he asked Haydn who had been snooping through his papers. Haydn explained that he merely organized them so Joseph would not be angry at the mess and apologized if he'd gotten them out of order. George said he was sorry for snapping at him, but as Haydn now watched him tuck the finished papers into a file in his desk, he decided that next time, he would just leave the mess and let George deal with Joseph's temper.

Haydn had planned to go to the dress shop at lunch, but when the clock struck Noon, he was still too busy to take a break. He called Mildred and told her he would pick the dress up on his way home from work.

* * *

At Heckmann's Dress Shoppe, the pace was equally brisk, and Rina was glad when she finally got a break at the Noon hour. She told Mrs. Heckmann she was going to go to Klaussen's Dry Goods store to pick up supplies and get something to eat.

Klaussen's was both a dry goods and grocery store located on The Strand, just two blocks from the wharves. It could reasonably have been called a general store, but Johann Klaussen had started out simply in dry goods and had never bothered to change the name of the store.

Klaussen's offered a wide selection of goods, including shoes, tobacco, and produce, and it always smelled of coffee, thanks to a coffee roaster located next door. Rina loved the smell, and when she entered the store, she stood just inside the doorway for a moment taking in the aroma and warmth inside the store.

"Good afternoon, Miss Rina," Mr. Klaussen said from behind the main counter, located to the right of the front door. "It's too cold for a young lady to be running about, eh?"

"It cannot be helped," she said. "I need supplies for Mrs. Heckmann."

Rina walked to the long counter and leaned on it. Behind the counter was a wall of shelves with various clothing-related items—fabric, buttons, ready-made shoes, etc. She liked looking at all the items and imagining what she could make with them.

"Here is a list she gave me," she said, handing the old man a piece of paper. "You'll put this all on our account?"

"Of course."

"Hello, Rina." The voice of a young man drifted

over her shoulder. Rina turned to see a tall, thin young man with thick, blond hair, blue eyes and an innocent expression. He was wiping his hands on an apron. "Have you had a busy morning at the dress shop?"

"Hello, Frederick," she said. "Yes, you wouldn't believe all the gowns that have come in from Tuesday's parties. It's always this way after a big celebration night, though, so I guess I'm not surprised. Thank you for asking."

Rina could see him searching for something else to say, and she was about to rescue him and ask if he had enjoyed Barton Mills party as much as she had, but then he asked, "Will you have to work late?"

"Yes, I imagine so."

"I see," he said. "I thought I might call tonight, but I can wait until another evening."

"Thank you," Rina said and touched his arm. "I think that would be best. I'm still tired from the party on Tuesday, and I'm sure after a long day, I'll want nothing more than to eat a bit and go to sleep."

"I understand," Frederick said. "You looked lovely at the party."

"Thank you. And you looked very handsome."

Frederick beamed. "That was a new suit. I was going to offer to walk you home, but you left before I could ask," he said.

"That's very considerate," she said. She could sense

that he wanted her to say if someone else had escorted her home, but she didn't want to announce that she had been walking around alone, so she said nothing more.

"It's always best for a lady to be safely escorted," he said.

"Certainly," she said.

"Here are your items," Mr. Klaussen said handing a bundle to Rina. "Tell Mrs. Heckmann I'm happy to be of service."

"I will," said Rina. "Thank you."

She took the parcels and left, adding a quick, "Have a nice day," to Frederick.

* * *

Haydn closed his cash drawer and stretched his arms up.

"Okay, boys, that's it for today," Joseph announced. "Stefan, I'll see you tomorrow. George, you'll lock up?"

"Yes, sir."

"Father, don't forget I have to fetch Margaret's dress," Haydn said. "I might be a little late for dinner."

Joseph nodded, put on his coat and went out the front door.

"Good for you," Stefan said quietly to Haydn. "Take providence by the shoulders, my boy."

Haydn felt his face color, but he smiled, then went to

the door and put on his coat. He left the bank and walked the four blocks to Mrs. Heckmann's so fast he bordered on running. When he could see the shop, he slowed his pace and tried to even his breathing. When he got to the shop's door, he paused a moment, took a deep breath, then entered, trying to appear nonchalant.

"Good afternoon," he said to Mrs. Heckmann, who stood behind the counter writing in an account book. "I'm glad I arrived before you closed."

"You just caught us," she said, putting the book under the counter.

"I understand my sister's gown is ready. I brought it in yesterday."

"Yes, I remember," Mrs. Heckmann said. "I'll go get it."

As she pushed through the door leading to the workroom in back, Haydn craned his neck to see if he could catch a glimpse of the young woman he'd seen yesterday. He saw a flash of curly hair and thought it might be her, but the door closed before he could see a face. Moments later, the older woman pushed back through the door, carrying the dress.

"Here we are. Good as new," she said, handing it to him.

"Wonderful, thank you." He hesitated, trying to think how he might stall for time. He had to get a look at that girl.

"Is there anything else, Mr. Winters?"

He held up the dress and pretended to inspect the bottom of the dress. "You did repair the hem, didn't you?"

"Yes, sir. We certainly did."

"Can you show me where? I'm not sure where I should be looking to check the repair."

Mrs. Heckmann looked surprised. "Men aren't usually so interested in our work," she said. "But I'll call the seamstress for you. She'll be happy to show you where the repair was done." She pushed open the workroom door and shouted, "Rina!"

Haydn held his breath.

Then she was there. The girl from the beach, the one he'd seen yesterday, in this very shop!

The young woman stepped through the door from the workroom, pushing curls away from her face, and Haydn almost audibly sucked in his breath. She was beautiful! He'd seen Tuesday night that she was attractive, but the moon didn't do her justice. At first, she didn't look at Haydn, her attention focused on her employer.

"Yes, Mrs. Heckmann? Is something the matter?"

"Rina, can you show Mr. Winters where you repaired the hem on this dress?"

She looked at the young man and a look of faint recognition registered on her face. Haydn could see that she was trying to place him, and he was almost hoping she wouldn't remember where she had seen him.

"Of course," she said, reaching for the dress. "Is there something wrong with it? I'm sure I repaired all of the tear." She inspected the section of hem that she had repaired.

"I'm sure you did a fine job," he said, a wide smile on his face. "I just thought I should double-check that it was done. I wouldn't want my mother to have to send me all the way back again tomorrow. It looks perfect, though. Thank you."

Haydn tipped his hat, took the dress and backed toward the door. He stepped into the street, the shop's bell tinkling.

After he'd disappeared out the door, the two women looked at each other with raised eyebrows.

"That was strange," Rina said.

"I never question the ways of the rich," Mrs. Heckmann said, waving her hand. "Particularly when it's a customer. If he'd asked me to put the dress on, I wouldn't have blinked an eye." Rina laughed, but she knew Mrs. Heckmann had thought it was as strange as she did.

She tried to think where she had seen the handsome, young man before, but she couldn't imagine where their paths would have crossed other than the store, and she was tired. She'd figure it out later.

"Will that be all, Mrs. Heckmann?" Rina asked. "I think I've finished all the dresses you had for me today."

"Then off with you," Mrs. Heckmann said.

A few minutes later, Rina stepped out of the shop and onto the sidewalk. She hoped she wouldn't run into Frederick on the way home. She had told him she'd have to work late so he wouldn't call tonight. She had seen him socially at the party on Tuesday, and that was enough for one week.

She liked Frederick, but she could tell he wanted to court her, and she wasn't interested in him in that way. He was a kind, gentle young man with a good job, and he was just the kind of person that her father wanted her to marry. In fact, he was *the* person her father wanted her to marry. But Frederick was too simple. He wasn't stupid. But he was simple. Simple and practical.

Rina, on the other hand, had dreams—dreams she might never accomplish or even follow, but they were important to her. She fantasized about designing magnificent costumes for the grandest theater companies in the world, working with only the most luxurious fabrics, traveling the world, and dressing opera stars. She dreamed of being part of that magic world of theater, creating the illusion that people paid to lose themselves in. She dreamed of leaving this tiny little island and exploring the world's greatest cities, then coming back home and sharing with her father all she'd seen and done.

She had big, impractical dreams.

And she wanted to be able to share those dreams with the man she would marry. She wanted that man to listen and hear and understand, even if nothing could ever come of it. And Frederick, for all his goodness, just didn't seem like someone who would understand all of that.

But he was someone who could get his feelings hurt if he knew she had lied to him, and she didn't want to do that. So she scanned the street from the doorway to make sure Frederick was nowhere in sight. Seeing that the coast was clear, she stepped out onto the sidewalk and had just taken a few steps, when Haydn appeared from an alley next to the shop.

"Hello," he said.

Rina's breath caught and she jumped.

"I'm so sorry!" Haydn said. "I didn't mean to scare you."

Rina held her hand against her chest. "Well, that didn't quite work out, then," she said. "Was there something else you needed with the dress?"

"No, the dress is fine," he said, lifting his arm, which had the dress draped over it. "I think you don't remember me. Perhaps you'd recognize me if I started talking to myself." He stepped back and did a pantomime of his performance on the beach the night before, causing Margaret's dress to flail about.

Rina gasped, then raised her hand to her mouth to

muffle a laugh.

"Ah, yes," she said, her eyes sparking with recognition. "I remember now. I thought you looked familiar."

He wasn't doing much to assuage her fears about his sanity with this performance, but something told her he was probably just unsophisticated about women rather than unbalanced. And unsophisticated she could deal with. She started walking, and Haydn fell in step beside her.

"I'm afraid I made a terrible spectacle of myself the other night," he said. "I hope I didn't drive you to the authorities!"

"No, I didn't think you were quite worthy of police action. Besides, it's likely that on Mardi Gras night the police would've ignored any calls about a man acting strangely."

"True, true," Haydn said, nodding. "Well, next time I want to figure out the world's problems, I'll find some place less crowded."

Less crowded than an empty beach in the middle of the night? Rina thought.

"Not that you were crowding me," he said. "I just meant…I mean, I just thought that…you see I was trying to think through something, and I thought the fresh air and calming sound of the sea might help me think. There's something about the moon over the water." She saw his brow knit and his lips purse with discomfort.

"I understand completely," Rina said, and her voice made it clear that she did. "I often walk along the beach or sit on the dunes and watch the gulls or listen to the waves when I need some solitude or quiet. It's a wonderful place for thinking." She saw his face relax.

"Yes," he said. He exhaled, and she realized he'd been holding his breath. "That's it. That's what I meant."

They locked eyes for a second. Haydn then broke eye contact and spoke abruptly.

"Well, I don't usually run errands for my mother, but I was glad that I did this time," he said. "I was just sure yesterday that I recognized you."

"So, you came back to be sure?" Rina said, raising her eyebrows.

"Yes."

"And then you waited for me to leave the shop to be doubly sure?"

"No, I waited for you to leave so I could apologize for last night and properly introduce myself. My name is Haydn," he said and bowed slightly.

"My name is Rina," she said. She thought the gesture looked courtly, and it made her smile. Maybe he wasn't so unsophisticated after all.

"Rina," Haydn repeated as they started walking. "Do you walk this way every day, Rina?"

"Well, yes," she giggled. "This is my route home

from work."

"Of course," he said, his cheeks coloring. "Perhaps I can walk you home again sometime, then."

"You haven't walked me home this time," she said.

"True," he said. "Shall I walk you home, then?"

"Another time," she said.

"Another time then. But I'll hold you to it," Haydn said. He stopped walking and tipped his hat to her. She kept walking and after several steps, she glanced back over her shoulder. He was still standing there, watching her walk away. She felt a rush in her chest, and she turned her head back quickly.

CHAPTER 7

APRIL 20, 1900

The day after Haydn officially met Rina at Mrs. Heckmann's shop, he had waited for her outside the shop at the end of the day. She had again refused to let him walk her all the way home, but she told him that she often took walks along the beach during her lunch hour.

So, the next day, Haydn went to the beach at lunch. He had to walk around for a bit, unsure exactly where she walked, but he eventually found her sitting on a dune, eating an apple. He smiled and approached her.

"Well, Miss Rina, fancy meeting you here."

"Mr. Winters, how nice to see you," she said and stood, wiping the sand from her skirt. "I was just about to walk back to work. Would you care to join me?"

For the next two months, they met at the beach, usually for lunch, though lately they had started to meet at other times as well—after work or in the evening after a night out with friends.

In some moments, when he was with Rina, Haydn felt like time was standing still. In others, it seemed to flash by like a lightning strike. He couldn't believe he had only known Rina for two months. He felt like he'd known her all his life. Yet when he was with her, it felt like he barely greeted her before it was time to kiss her goodbye. They had just now sat down on a dune, sandwiches in hand, and he was already dreading leaving. He gazed at her.

"You know, you're the person I've known the shortest amount of time in my life, but it seems like you know me better than anyone I've ever known," he said.

"Oh, I don't think that can be true," she said. "It sounds like you and your friend Will are fast friends. I'm sure he knows you much better than I do."

"Well, he knows more about me in some ways, because we've been friends for so long, but it's different with you. Remember when I told you about my dog, and how I had found him last month when it was raining, huddling under a bush, wet and shivering?"

"That was so sad," Rina said. "But it was so sweet of you to make the little shelter for him with pieces of wood and leaves."

"Well, when I told Will about it, the first thing he said was, 'He must have smelled terrible! Nothing worse than a wet dog.' And when I said that I was more concerned about him being wet and cold, his response was, 'That's what dogs do. They live outside.'"

"That's rather callous." Rina said, frowning.

"Exactly. You and I are the same. I don't have to explain to you how I felt. You just know, because you would feel the same way. When I tell you something that happened, and how I responded, I don't have to justify it, because you make me feel like whatever I've felt or done was the most logical or reasonable possible reaction. The only other person who has ever treated me like that was my Nana."

Since Nana died, Haydn had felt that he was some sort of defective bird, trying to fly with the flock around him, but never quite reaching the right altitude. He was always too low or too high, and no one could ever quite see or hear him clearly. He felt alone and isolated in a crowded sky. But now there was Rina.

Rina flew beside him, as if the currents of the wind somehow tied her to him. She knew when he would dive, swoop, or land. She followed his every turn, his every change of direction, without needing explanation or warning. His movements were the movements she would have made even without him. He no longer had to try to do or be anything.

What he was, was exactly what she expected him to be, and it was all that she asked him to be. He took her hand and squeezed it, silently praying he would never have to be without her.

"I feel the same way," she said, squeezing his hand back.

When he first met her, Haydn decided not to tell anyone of his new romance. If his mother knew, she would do all in her power to break up the relationship, deeming Rina beneath him. If his friends knew, they would roll their eyes that he was back in the soup again with another woman. And George would just tease him and might let it slip to his mother.

So, he felt it was best to just keep the affair to himself so he could enjoy it without interference. The only person who knew Rina even existed was Stefan, since he had known about the romance since before it began. And Stefan was the soul of discretion.

Looking at Rina's beautiful face now, holding her warm hand, he wanted to shout to the mountaintops that he loved her. He actually felt it start to rise up through his stomach and into his chest. He straightened his back, in preparation for the big gust of breath the declaration would take, but then, when it reached his throat, it stuck there, and no sound came out. Instead, tears came to his eyes, and he looked away.

He was sure Rina had remained similarly mum with

her friends and family about the romance, though Haydn never asked her reasons. She hadn't asked him his, so he did not ask hers. And in this moment, unable to shout his feelings to the world, he felt unworthy of asking. So, instead he stood and wiped his eyes.

Rina stood and shook sand from her skirts. Haydn then took her by the shoulders, leaned into her, pressing his lips against her hair just above her ear and whispered, "I love you."

He heard her breath catch, then she said, "I love you, too." He embraced her fully for a few short seconds, then walked quickly away from the dune and back to the bank.

When Haydn walked into the bank, he saw that Joseph and George were still out to lunch. Stefan looked at Haydn.

"You had a nice lunch?"

"Very," Haydn said.

"Really? Very? That sounds like a lunch I might like to hear more about."

Haydn took his seat next to Stefan and unlocked his teller drawer. He was so relieved to have Stefan to talk to. If he didn't tell someone about his feelings for Rina, he thought he might explode.

"I told her I loved her," he blurted.

"Well," Stefan said, nodding. "You did have a big lunch, didn't you? What did she say?"

"She said she loves me, too."

"That is good."

"Yes," Haydn said. "I was a little sick when the words first came out. I thought, what if she doesn't say it back? But then she did!"

"So, what now?" Stefan asked.

Haydn pursed his lips. "I'm not sure. I know what I want to do. I want to marry her. But I also know that my mother will never stand for it."

Stefan nodded but said nothing. Haydn felt disappointed seeing the gesture. He'd wanted Stefan to contradict him—to tell him that Mildred would surely come around eventually.

"So, where does that leave us?" he continued. "If I marry her, my mother will make her feel like a trespasser. But if I don't marry her, life won't be worth living!"

Stefan raised an eyebrow.

"I know, that sounds dramatic, but I'm serious, Stefan. What's the point of anything if you can't be with the girl you love?"

"I understand," Stefan said and patted his shoulder.

"Do you? I mean, have you ever been in love?"

"Of course," Stefan said. "I was even married for a short time."

"You were?" Haydn was incredulous. How did he not know this? "When? Who was she?"

"She was a girl I went to school with. We were very

young, and very much in love." Stefan smiled. "She had the most wonderful chestnut hair and a laugh that made anyone around her start laughing, too."

"What happened?"

"Cholera."

Haydn pursed his lips and looked down, and the two men sat in silence for a few moments. Then Haydn asked hesitantly, "Was this here or before you came to the United States?"

"Here, my boy. I grew up in Galveston, just like you. Have I never told you that?"

"No," Haydn said with wide eyes. "I just assumed you came here as a young man and started working for my father."

"No, no," Stefan said, shaking his hand. "My father brought my mother and I here in 1845. You've heard of The Society for the Protection of German Immigrants to Texas?"

Haydn shook his head.

"The Adelsverein, or Verein?"

"Oh, the Verein, yes, I've heard of that. But I admit I don't really know what it is."

"The Verein was founded by 20 German noblemen, including five princes," Stefan said, holding up his right hand with the fingers extended. "They hoped that by encouraging immigration to Texas, they could provide opportunity for some of Germany's poor to improve their situations, while opening new markets for German products. Some even hoped to establish Texas as a sort of German state."

"Hmph," Haydn said. "I'm not sure that sounds so good."

"Well, they helped pay for thousands of Germans to come here, including my family. But unfortunately, the noblemen vastly underestimated the costs of the venture. Most of them had little business experience, so the society began to run out of money soon after it began sending people to Texas."

"Uh, oh," Haydn said.

"Yes. But they didn't let a little thing like running out of money stop them from continuing to send people," Stefan said with a raised eyebrow. "They just kept putting people on ships, and then when they—when *we* got to Texas, the Verein did not have the funds to properly provide for us."

"What was supposed to happen when people got here?"

"The Verein told people in Germany that upon arriving in Texas, they would be taken to New Braunfels, a settlement in the interior of the state, where they would be given land and supported for the first year, until their first crops came in. Instead, when we arrived at Indian Point, we were stranded."

"Where is Indian Point?"

"You know it now as Indianola. Before the storm of 1875, it was Indian Point, and it was second only to Galveston as the primary port for the state. It would have been a logical spot to bring people if you planned on sending them on to the interior of the state."

"But that didn't happen?"

"No. The Verein had enough money to feed us for a few months, but not to transport us any further. And after six weeks of living in a tent with little to do but pray we would not catch the dysentery that was spreading through the camp, my father had had enough.

"He told my mother that we were not going to New Braunfels. He said he had told her we would come to Texas, and we had. We would now make our way to Galveston, one way or another, and that would be that. And…that was that."

"And you've lived here ever since?"

"Every day," Stefan said.

Joseph and George came through the front door, and Haydn, who had been leaning on the counter, enthralled by Stefan's story, straightened up.

"Gentlemen," Joseph nodded to Stefan and Haydn. "Anything happen while we were out that I should know about?"

"No, sir," Haydn said.

"Good," Joseph said. "And as long as I have your attention, Haydn, I want you to come straight home after work today. No fooling around. I don't know what you've been doing lately after work, but George and I have plans with Mildred and Margaret to attend the opera tonight, so dinner needs to be on time this evening, and you know that your mother won't allow any of us to take a bite until everyone is in their chairs. So I expect to see you planted in yours at precisely six o'clock. Understood?"

"Yes, sir," Haydn said.

CHAPTER 8

APRIL 20, 1900

The rest of the day passed quickly for Rina. The dress shop was busy, and she did not want to be late leaving work. Her friend Melanie would be walking her home today so they could coordinate their plans for the evening.

When she had cleaned up her work materials, she left the shop in a rush of skirts, her hair slipping from its topknot.

"Have you been waiting long?" she asked Melanie when she met her at the corner.

"No, just a few minutes. We should hurry, though. I want to take my time getting ready for tonight. And I can see that your hair will need some work."

Rina tilted her chin down and looked at Melanie, as if peering over a pair of glasses. "You're very humorous," she said.

"I'm just thinking of you," Melanie said. "You're never going to find a husband running around the streets looking like a maniac. Speaking of finding a husband, will Frederick be there?"

"I assume so," Rina said. "He works as a waiter for most of the dances these days. And what do you win if you find me a husband?"

"Well, I don't want to be the only old married lady in this friendship. I need someone to swap stories with. And yes, I've noticed that Frederick has been working the dances lately," Melanie said, raising her eyebrows. "He must be working extra jobs to save up money for something special."

"Maybe his mean old employer doesn't pay him enough to buy whatever it is he wants," Rina said.

"He's paid well enough for a bachelor," Melanie said. "But maybe he's looking to change that situation."

"Aren't you the subtle one?"

"I can't afford to be subtle. You don't seem to take hints."

"So stop pushing them on me," Rina said and gave Melanie a push on her arm.

Frederick had a good job at Klaussen's Dry Goods, the store owned by Melanie's father. Rina agreed that

Frederick would be a good husband for someone, just not her. And she was sure that she would feel this way even if she weren't in love with someone else.

Rina knew there was probably no future in the affair with Haydn. Men like him didn't marry girls like her. She knew that. So, there was no point telling Melanie and getting her all excited or, worse, upsetting her. Rina didn't want to hear any lectures from her best friend about possibly losing out on a "real" relationship with Frederick for a frivolous romance with a rich boy.

Maybe this wasn't "real" in the way that everyone else would see it, but it was sure real to her. It was possibly the most real thing that had happened to her since her mother died. When Haydn touched her hand, it sent shocks through her. When he put his arm around her, she felt like she was safe from any storm. And when he kissed her, she felt like a warm wave of feathers moved down from her chest, through her stomach and into her privates. This afternoon, when he told her loved her, she could hardly breathe.

She knew that this whole episode might be a wonderful dream she would wake up from any moment, so she wanted to experience every second of it fully. Because when Haydn was gone, she would be left with nothing but memories for the rest of her life. There would never be another Haydn for her, so she wanted as much of him as she could have for as long as she could have him.

And that was certainly not a sentiment she could share with anyone. Ever. Good girls didn't entertain impossible romances. She couldn't even hope for anyone else's understanding, much less approval. So, she wouldn't seek it. She would make her memories now. And when Haydn was gone, she would settle for whatever life, and whatever husband, the Island would let her have. Or maybe there wouldn't be a husband—maybe she'd end up living that life of travel and excitement she wanted so deeply.

However it worked out, though, she would be content with the memories that no one could ever take from her.

"Look, let's just have fun tonight," Rina said.

"We'll be at the Garten Verein. Of course we'll have a good time!" Melanie said.

Garten Verein, or Garden Club in English, was a social club founded in 1876 at Avenue O and 27th Street by prosperous Galveston Germans. The five-acre club featured an antebellum home, now used as a clubhouse and dining room, walking paths, bowling alleys, tennis courts, a fountain and an octagon-shaped dancing pavilion with a cupola. Membership to the club was open to any German who could pay the $10 membership fee and $1.50 monthly dues.

Rina's father was not one of those people. His job at

the brewery did not afford such a luxury expense. But Melanie's father could pay it, and Melanie frequently brought Rina to the club's dances as a guest.

"I have to say, Rina, that I'm not sure how the presence of a handsome young man who adores you could be anything but a pleasure." Rina shot her best friend a look of annoyance, but Melanie continued. "You know, he may end up helping Daddy manage the store."

"That would be wonderful for him," Rina said. "But it has nothing to do with me."

"You used to seem kind of interested in Frederick."

"I've never really been interested in him. Not like that," Rina shrugged.

Melanie raised her eyebrows, as if to say, "Oh really?" but Rina pretended not to notice. Frederick had wanted to marry Rina since he was 14 and she was 12. She had entertained the thought of marrying him when she was younger and knew nothing of real love, but the prospect wasn't even a possibility now. She was sure she would always feel a gentle affection for Frederick, but she knew now that she would never feel for him the passion of real love.

She had tried to tell him once that he should direct his efforts toward a more willing subject. He had been flirting with her in his gentle way when she had come to the store for supplies. She had told him, "Frederick, you deserve a woman who will love you as you love her."

He had responded with unwavering faith, "You will, Katarina. You will."

She hadn't said more at the time, not wanting to hurt his feelings. But she knew the time would come when she would have to. With Frederick, Melanie, and her father all pushing for the same thing, she couldn't avoid the situation forever. Sooner or later, something painful was going to happen. But she didn't want to think about that now.

"What are you going to wear tonight, Melanie?"

"My striped dress."

"When are you going to let my grandmother and me make you something new?" Rina asked.

"John likes my dancing dress," Melanie said defensively.

"John would adore you if you wore sack cloth."

Melanie beamed. She and John planned to marry in the fall, and she knew Rina was right.

"What about you?" she asked Rina.

"I'm thinking of my blue dress."

"And you say you're not trying to earn a proposal tonight? With that dress, you may just get several."

"Really, Melanie, the way you go on," Rina said, blushing.

"I'm just truthful," Melanie said.

Rina was almost sorry that they had arrived at her house. Besides Haydn, there was no one else she'd rather spend time with than her best friend. Melanie was kind, funny, and warm, and Rina was grateful to have such a good friend. She wished she could share everything about Haydn with Melanie, but if she couldn't, she was glad to know that if she couldn't have Haydn for a lifetime, she could have Melanie. She reached out and seized Melanie in a hug.

"Well!" Melanie said. When Rina released her she asked, "What was that for?"

"Nothing special. I just thought your dress needed some wrinkling."

"Well, good job then," Melanie said, smoothing her dress. "Are you sure everything is alright?"

"Everything is grand," Rina said. "I'll see you tonight. You'll come by and get me?"

"Of course," Melanie said. She waved a hand and walked away, heading in the direction of her home.

CHAPTER 9

APRIL 20, 1900

Just after 7pm, Jefferson pulled the Winters carriage up to the entrance of the Grand Opera House. George stepped out of the carriage first and looked up at the front archway of the four-story Romanesque Revival-style building. The structure was only six years old and stood as a testament to Galveston's position as a leader financially and culturally in the state, the country, and even the world, as Islanders saw it.

The Winters family had seen a number of internationally famous performers at the Grand, and anyone who was anyone in Galveston society had box seats and was seen there for any major performance.

George helped his mother and Margaret out of the

carriage then held the door for them as Joseph exited and told Jefferson when to return for the family. The four climbed the grand staircase to the lobby and looked around the room.

There weren't a lot of people there yet, but Margaret spotted her friend Emma and abandoned them.

"Emma, thank God," Margaret said, throwing her hands up. "I just got here, and I'm already bored. Tell me something fun!"

Emma giggled and George watched them wander off to talk about God knows what. He looked at his pocket watch. Five past 7:00pm. He sighed. He knew he should be used to the fact that Mildred liked to arrive early to greet acquaintances in the lobby before going to the family's box seat to the right of the stage, but he found it tedious to listen to Mildred and her cronies.

"Mildred, how lovely to see you," Anna Martin said, approaching the foursome.

"And you as well, Anna," Mildred said. "Your gown is divine."

The ladies launched into a discussion about spring fashions, and George and Joseph peeled away. George went to a bar that served patrons before performances and at intermission and ordered a drink. When he took his glass from the bartender, he saw that Joseph had found a colleague to discuss business with, and he walked in the opposite direction. He spotted a familiar face.

"Beatrice!" he said, approaching her and kissing her on the cheek. "You smashing girl. I didn't know you'd be here tonight."

"Oh, George, hello. I didn't know you'd be here either," Beatrice said. She fingered a strand of pearls, and her eyes darted around the lobby. "Are you here with your family?"

"Who else?" he asked. "Can I get you a drink?"

"No, but thank you," she said.

Lloyd Preston joined the pair with two drinks. He handed one to Beatrice.

"Lloyd!" George said. "Well, the gang's all here tonight, aren't we?"

"Yes, it appears we are," Lloyd smiled.

"Who dragged you down here, Preston? Is your sister here with that sod husband of hers, Harold?" George said looking around.

"Yes, they're here," Lloyd said, glancing at Beatrice. "We're all together tonight."

"Well, maybe we can all go find something fun to do when this is all over," George suggested.

"Oh...well," Lloyd hesitated. "I believe we have plans after this."

"Yes," Beatrice said, looking George in the eye. "We do."

The three stood in an uneasy silence as George grasped the situation. When he allowed the facts to take root in his mind, heat washed over his face and ears.

"Oh, right," he finally said, his smile tight. "I must be daft. You're *together*. Of course. Well, you don't need me to crowd things up, now do you? You two kids go on, then. Things are probably about to start. And I need another drink," he said and drained his glass.

Lloyd put his hand on Beatrice's elbow to lead her into the theater, and she reached out and touched George's arm.

"We'll talk later," she said in a low voice.

"Nothing to talk about, my girl," he said. She looked at him hard, but said nothing.

* * *

"So you escaped opera night?" Will asked Haydn. The two sat in the parlor of Edward Billingsley's home, where they played cards most Friday nights with Edward and Peter Martin.

"Yes, it is the one great advantage to being the 'extra' son—no opera obligation!" Haydn said. Opera was his mother's passion. She had even named Haydn for her favorite composer, Franz Joseph Haydn, but he had never cared much for classical music. He was partial to Ragtime, though Mildred had made it clear that such low-brow music was not to be played on her phonograph.

"George has to go, because as Father's protégé, he

must mingle with the 'important' people," Haydn said. "I am not important, and therefore, must mingle with you swine."

"Bacon is delicious," Will said.

Edward entered the room and handed Will a glass of beer. "You have bacon?"

"Why would I have bacon?" Will took the beer and gulped a big swallow, leaving him with a foam mustache.

"You were talking about bacon," Edward said. "Doesn't seem fair to talk about it if you don't have any."

"Life isn't fair," Will said.

"When is Peter getting here?" Haydn asked. "If we don't start playing soon, we'll be playing all night."

"Well, if Peter doesn't get here soon, we'll give up on the cards, and I'll tell the cook to rustle up some oysters, and we'll just feast," Edward said.

"Forget the oysters," Will said. "I want bacon now."

"Hello, boys! Sorry I'm late!" Peter announced as he entered the parlor.

"You bastard," Will said. "Billingsley was about to come up with bacon. Or oysters. You could've been late by a few more minutes."

"We'll eat both while we play," Peter said. "Now, sit down and someone deal the cards."

* * *

"Oh, my darling daughter, you are a beauty fit for the stage," Gustaf Schmidt said to Rina as she primped in front of a mirror by the front door. Her hair was piled on top of her head, a bun surrounded by a large poof.

"Thank you, Papa. I think you may be prejudiced, though."

"Nonsense, you look just like your mother, God rest her soul. She would have burst with pride seeing you all dressed up."

"It's just a dance," Rina said, though she loved when her father told her that she looked like her mother. Gustaf waved his hand in dismissal. In a rocking chair in the middle of the room, Rina's grandmother smiled her approval at Rina.

"What do you think, Oma? Do I look like Mama?"

"The image, liebschen."

Rina smiled and looked again at the mirror. She imagined her mother standing next to her, fussing with her dress or her hair. She wished her mother were here now, and she could talk to her about Haydn. In her imagination, her mother was the kind of person who would understand anything and take her side no matter what. She knew that if her mother were really here, she probably wouldn't be that unconditional. But in her mind, her mother could be anything she wanted her to be.

"Will Frederick be there?" Gustaf asked.

A knock at the door signaled Melanie's arrival.

"Rescued from nosey questions!" Rina said opening the door. Gustaf harrumphed.

"Hello Mr. Schmidt," Melanie said nodding to Rina's father. She turned to Rina's grandmother. "Mrs. Gruebber."

"Hello, my dear," Gustaf said. "The two most beautiful girls in Galveston!"

Melanie giggled. Rina went over and kissed her father on the cheek.

"I love you, Papa."

"Be careful and have fun, schatze. I love you, too." He hugged her, and the girls descended the stairs and climbed into the Klaussen's handsome cab. Rina saw Mr. Klaussen nod at her father, who was watching from the front door and returned the gesture.

The girls talked animatedly about plans for Melanie and John's wedding on the ride to Garten Verein.

"I intend to do all the beadwork and lace on your dress myself," said Rina.

"I was hoping you would. I love Mrs. Heckmann and Mrs. Werner, but your detail work is so much better. You have such a talent, Rina."

"Oh, I don't know about that. I think I just have youth on the other two ladies."

Melanie shook her head. "It's more than that. You could work as a costumer, Rina, really you could. You could work with one of the traveling plays or opera companies."

"That would be wonderful. Of course, if I did travel with an opera, Papa would have to give up his plan of me marrying a good German boy on the island and raising lots of children that he can spoil. So maybe I should look into it."

"Nonsense," Mrs. Klaussen chimed in. "That sounds like a perfectly wonderful plan to me. Melanie is going to give Mr. Klaussen and I lots of grandchildren to dote on, aren't you child?"

"Mother!" Melanie hissed.

The coach approached the Victorian-style dancing pavilion. When it came to a stop, Melanie and Rina exited the carriage and entered the pavilion.

"You wouldn't really want to leave Galveston, would you, Rina?" Melanie asked as they stepped inside.

"If it was for a good reason, I would," Rina said. She knew that it was unlikely she would ever leave the island, but she liked to hope that it was a possibility. She had nothing against Galveston. It's just that she had never been anywhere else, and she longed to see more. And meeting Haydn had taught her that anything could happen.

"Like joining an opera company?" Melanie asked.

"Maybe," Rina said. "Life can be unexpected. Who knows what may be in store for me someday?"

The two found their way to a table of friends. The

table featured a pitcher of punch in the center and all the seats around the table were taken, but when Rina and Melanie arrived, everyone squeezed together, and John commandeered two more seats from another table.

"Look at you," he said and kissed Melanie on the cheek. "And Rina if you'll sit on the other side of me, every man in here will wish he were me."

"True, but if I sit next to you instead of Melanie, I'll have to lean across you to gossip."

"The lady makes a point," he said and seated the girls next to one another.

"Good evening," Frederick said, approaching the table with additional glasses. He placed the glasses on the tabled and gazed at Rina. "Is there anything I can get you? More punch?"

"Hello, Frederick." Rina said. "More punch would be lovely."

When they first entered the Pavilion, Rina had seen Frederick on the other side of the room, so she knew that their table wasn't one of the ones he was responsible for serving. She wondered if he had switched assignments with one of the other waiters upon seeing her sit down or simply commandeered the table. She was flattered, even though she knew she shouldn't show it. She didn't want to encourage his affection if she couldn't return it.

The evening proceeded with much dancing and laughing. At the height of the fun, the girls at the table asked questions about Melanie and John's wedding and cooed over her engagement ring. John's friends ribbed him, and he warned them that any one of them could be next.

"You're not safe," he warned them. "The girls have plans for each of you. What do you think they're doing when they all go to the powder room together? They're comparing battle plans."

The girls howled protest, and the men made oaths never to be taken. John put his arm around Melanie and squeezed. Rina said that on that note, she needed some water and excused herself from the table.

She walked to a table set with glasses of water. The waiters stood behind the table, keeping an eye on their tables and keeping the water glasses filled. Frederick moved to where Rina drank slowly from one of the glasses.

"Your dress is breathtaking," he said.

"Thank you. And you look very handsome in your waiter's costume," she said. She realized as soon as she said it, though, that it sounded flirtatious, and she silently chastised herself. "Do they have new jackets this season?"

"Yes, they do," he said. "They're a little shorter than the old ones. I can't decide if I like them better or not."

"Maybe you just need to wear it more often to decide. You could wear it to the store tomorrow."

"Oh, I couldn't do that," he said with a serious look.

"Mr. Klaussen would never—. Oh, you're teasing me." Rina laughed, and he dropped his eyes to the floor.

She put her hand on his arm and said, "Just a little. The jackets really are very nice."

She took her hand away, and they stood, watching people dance. She wanted to say something, but she wasn't sure what, and the truth is, she didn't want to drag out the conversation, so she finally said, "Well, I'll have to come to the store tomorrow for some supplies, so I'll see you then?"

"Oh yes. Of course," he said.

She set down her half-empty glass of water and returned to her friends, relieved to be back at the table.

"Who is ready to dance some more?" she challenged.

CHAPTER 10

APRIL 20, 1900

George stood in the lobby, staring out of one of the windows. He heard the opera break for intermission, and he turned to see Mildred emerge from the theater almost immediately and move swiftly toward him. He turned back toward the window.

"There you are," she said. "What are you doing? You haven't even been inside yet."

"I'm fine, mother," George said with a slur. He saw Mildred glare at him in the window reflection.

"I didn't ask you how you were," she said. She put a hand on his shoulder and turned him around to face her. "And I can see that you are not fine. You are drunk, right here in the lobby of the Grand Opera House. And I won't have it. You don't have to go in to see the opera, but you cannot sit out here and get drunk. It is unseemly. If you're going to make a spectacle of yourself, leave this building right now, before you embarrass me or your father."

The lobby began to fill with people.

"Thank you for your concern," George said. He tossed back the rest of his drink and set the glass down hard on a small table next to the window. "It warms my heart."

George looked past his mother and saw Beatrice, Lloyd, Harold, and Daisy enter the lobby talking animatedly.

"Well, if it isn't the happy couple," George said too loudly. ·

Everyone in the lobby turned and looked at him. Daisy blushed, and Beatrice stared at George stone-faced. Harold walked up to him.

"George, old boy, glad to see you," he said, trying to shield George from the view of Beatrice and Lloyd as well as blocking the view of the other patrons in the lobby.

"I'm sure it is," George said angrily. "I'm sure you're just thrilled to run into me tonight."

"George," Harold said in a low voice, "I know this is awkward. Really, I do. But this isn't the place."

"Isn't it?" George said, his voice growing even louder. "Why, this is the public debut of Galveston's newest society couple. Isn't this the place to discuss their budding romance?"

Beatrice stalked over, her head held erect and her knuckles white, as she clutched a fan in her fist.

"George, I told you I would talk to you later," she said. "I will not do this—not here and not now. You go home and sleep it off. Until you do, I have nothing to say to you."

She turned and walked back to Lloyd and Daisy, took Lloyd's arm and ushered him to another part of the lobby. Harold patted George on the shoulder, then rejoined Daisy, Beatrice, and Lloyd.

Mildred looked at George with barely contained rage, then walked purposefully back into the theater. George started toward the stairs, but before he reached them, a hand clasped his shoulder.

"Rough night, Winters?" The voice was nasal. George wheeled around and looked into flat, brown eyes. The man was as tall as George, but more solidly built. His hair was dark and curly, his teeth crooked, and he wore a large mustache.

"Mr. Reynolds," George said. "Hello. I didn't expect to see you here."

"It would appear your evening is just full of surprises," Vincent Reynolds said, smiling with amusement for an instant, then turning serious. "Since you have not responded to my other inquiries, though, I should think that running into me would not be a surprise. I should think you would be expecting to run into me…or more accurately, for me to run into you. Did you think you would be able to avoid me, Mr. Winters? When a man is in my debt, I am everywhere. I am a ghost."

George didn't know what to say.

"Do you have my money?" the man asked, digging his fingers into George's shoulder.

"No, sir, I'm sorry, not on my person," George winced. "As I said, I didn't expect to see you."

"What a pity. Perhaps I should go in and ask your mother for the money. She seems so interested in your affairs. Box A, is it?"

"No!" George said. He tried to compose himself. "I mean, please don't bother her. She's very taken with the opera." George no longer felt drunk. His head was beginning to hurt, but his senses felt sharp.

"I want my money now, Mr. Winters."

"I can get it. I have it. At home."

"Which does not help me in my need for the money now, does it?"

"I can go get it for you. Right now. I can be back before the second half of the show is over," George said. His voice had a pleading tone that he didn't like, but he couldn't control it.

Reynolds appeared to mull the offer. After an

excruciating five seconds, he stepped close to George and began to straighten George's bow tie.

"This is a favor I'm doing you, Mr. Winters. Do you understand that? It is a courtesy—one I shall not extend again. I'm going to go to my seat now, but if I exit this theater tonight, and my money is not in my pocket, I shall break whatever part of your body I'm in the mood to see bent, and then I'll send an associate to your home. He will collect what you owe me from whomever he encounters, perhaps in trade. That sister of yours has become quite the beautiful young lady." He pressed the tie into George's throat, which had contracted in anger when Reynolds mentioned Margaret.

"Is that clear, Mr. Winters?"

Rage thudding in his ears, George said nothing.

"I said, 'Is that clear, Mr. Winters?'" Reynolds said, pushing his thumbs into George's throat.

"Yes," George coughed.

"Good." Reynolds released George's tie and straightened his own. "If I were you, Mr. Winters, I'd hurry. This opera doesn't seem to be holding my attention. I can't be sure how much longer I shall stay." He picked up a walking stick resting on the wall and turned to a large, tattooed man who had been waiting a few feet behind him.

"Show Mr. Winters that I'm serious, Jacques."

The large man grabbed George by the hair and

punched him hard in the stomach. He released his grip, and George doubled over and tried not to vomit on the carpet. Reynolds had already entered the theater before Jacques landed the punch.

"You better hurry," he told George in accented English.

Fear mixed with desperation, pain, and bourbon, and George felt nauseated and dizzy. His legs felt separate from his body, but they carried him down the stairs and out the front doors of the theater. He ran toward his house, stopping twice to vomit, then chastising himself for slowing down.

When he got to the house, he bolted up the stairs to his room. He counted the few dollars he had in his nightstand, cursed and ran to Haydn's room. A few weeks ago, he saw Haydn putting some bills into the top drawer of his dresser. He opened the drawer, dug under several pairs of clean underwear and found what he was looking for. He picked up a stack of cash, counted out the bills he needed and put the rest of the stack back, replacing the underwear and shutting the drawer.

George didn't know what Haydn was saving the money for, but whatever it was, it couldn't be as important as what George needed it for now. He promised himself he would replace the money as soon as his luck turned around and dashed out of the house.

When he returned to the Grand 20 minutes later, Jacques was waiting in the lobby.

"You got Mr. Reynolds' package?" the man asked.

"Yes. Should I wait for him out here?"

"You can give it to me. He don't want to talk to you no more tonight." He held out a hand.

George hesitated, then reluctantly handed him the money. What was to stop this man from pocketing the money and telling Reynolds that George had not paid, forcing George to pay again or suffer the consequences? But what choice did he have? The man counted the money.

"Next time, don't make us look for you."

"There won't be a next time," George said resolutely.

"There's always a next time," the man grinned, revealing yellow teeth.

CHAPTER 11

APRIL 20, 1900

At Garten Verein, when the last dance was over, Rina watched John kiss Melanie's hand and felt a small pang of jealousy. She wished Haydn were here to kiss her hand. She realized she probably looked wistful and put on a quick smile.

"What will you two do when you don't have to part at the end of an evening anymore?" Rina asked them.

"I'll never tell," John said, and both Rina and Melanie blushed.

The girls climbed into the Klaussen's coach. When they arrived at Rina's house, she climbed out of the cab and bid the family goodnight.

"Don't you want father to walk you to the door?"

Melanie asked.

"No, this is fine. No sense in both of us climbing stairs. But thank you again for a lovely evening. I really enjoyed the dance."

"Such a lovely girl," she heard Mrs. Klaussen say as they drove away.

Rina walked toward the stairs to her family's apartment, but when the coach was out of sight, she changed course.

A few minutes later, her boots crunched softly through wet sand. Haydn ran toward her and embraced her. He then stepped back and held her arms out.

"Look at you!" he said. "That dress is magnificent. You are magnificent in it."

"I don't think you can even see me," she said, feeling her face flush. "It's too dark."

"You light up the darkness. That night when I first saw you here, it was like the sun had awoken to illuminate only your face."

"I think the moon has made you senseless," Rina said.

"You're the only thing that's made sense to me in a long time." He touched her face, then leaned forward and kissed her softly. "So how much time do we have?"

"A half hour at most," she said. "Any longer and my father will worry."

Rina sat down, and Haydn dropped beside her. He

sat close, one leg straight out, touching hers, and the other bent.

"They're going to have to name this dune for us if we keep patronizing it, you know?" he asked.

"Oh, this has been my dune for a long time," Rina said. "I had it monogrammed, but the wind kept blowing it away. But it knows it's mine. It only allows you here by my permission. If you were here with another girl, it would cover you both mercilessly in sand."

"Is that so? Well, I shall make sure I never attempt that, then. The amount of sand I'm tracking home as it is raises eyebrows."

"Oh?" she asked.

"Oh, nothing to worry about," he said, waving his hand. "The servants have been complaining, so my mother tells me to stop tracking so much sand in, but she doesn't ask why there seems to be more than usual. That would require interest. And my father just says, 'It's an island, Mildred. Who doesn't track sand?'"

Rina laughed. "Well, at least you have your mother."

"That's true," Haydn said and put his arm around her waist. "Do you remember your mother at all?"

"Not really," Rina admitted. "Sometimes, I think I do, but I think I'm really just picturing what my grandmother has told me about her and convincing myself it's a memory."

"How old were you when she died?"

"Five. When we came here, I was three. My mother was an opera singer in Germany—really wonderful from what my grandmother says."

"Wow, really?"

"Yes, and my father was a master brewer. When my parents came to America in 1886, they had planned to go to San Antonio. Adolphus Busch built a large, mechanized brewery there, called the Lone Star Brewery, and Papa wanted to work there, but my parents thought my mother would have a better chance to sing in Galveston, so they came here instead."

"I hope it's not rude for me to ask, but what happened to your mother?"

"Two years after they moved to Galveston, she was stricken with cholera."

Haydn nodded slowly, and they sat in silence for a few minutes. Haydn seemed to be holding his breath, and Rina felt like he wanted to say something—a condolence maybe? But he didn't seem sure what to say. The breeze coming in across the waves pushed against her face, and she took a deep breath.

"I look like her," she said.

"Then clearly she was beautiful," Haydn let out his breath and squeezed her against his side.

"I think that's part of the reason my father would be so devastated if I left Galveston. It would be like losing her again."

Haydn eased his grip on her waist and looked up at the sky. "So you'd never leave Galveston?"

"It's not as if I wouldn't like to," she said. "If it were up to me, I'd travel the whole world! But I can't see how I can leave, really. Who would take care of my father and my grandmother?"

"Do they need taking care of?"

"Maybe not now. But someday they will, and with my mother gone, who else would there be but me? I have no brothers or sisters, and eventually my grandmother will be gone, and without me, my father would be totally alone. It would be selfish of me to leave."

Haydn said nothing for a bit, and finally Rina asked, "What about you? Would you leave Galveston?"

"It's not a question of would, but when," he said. "I'm going to Virginia in the fall to attend college, so if nothing else, I'll be gone several years for that. After that, I'm not sure where I'll go."

Rina felt a lump form in her throat. She tried to tell herself that she was being ridiculous—that she had known all along that there was no future in the romance. But some part of her had hoped that maybe there was a chance.

Hearing Haydn say that he would be leaving in a few months, though, made it crystal clear that there was, in fact, no chance. The time she had with him now was all the time she would ever have. She reached up and wiped away a tear before it could fall on her dress.

"Are you okay?" Haydn put his arm back around her.

"Yes, I'm just being sentimental," she said and turned her face away from him. "I get a little silly sometimes when I think about my mother."

He took her gently by the chin and turned her face to him then kissed her. She threw her arms around him and kissed him back passionately. He lay her down, and she pulled him against her. She arched her back, and his hand moved up her waist, across her ribs until briefly touching her breast through her dress. She gasped, and he pulled away abruptly.

"I'm so sorry," he panted. "I...I'm so sorry."

In the throws of the kiss, she had felt a mixture of desperation and desire, but now she felt fear and even a bit of shame. Would he reject her now? Would he push her away as a harlot? She knew that he had instigated the kiss, but would he think that she had been too eager?

Girls weren't supposed to encourage that kind of physical behavior. They were supposed to be coy. But she wasn't good at coy, and she didn't like pretending to feel something she didn't, or not to feel something she did, particularly when she knew now that her time with Haydn was limited. She wasn't sure what to do, so she simply said, "I should probably go."

"Yes, we both should probably get home," Haydn said. They stood and straightened their clothes. They stood awkwardly for a moment then Haydn kissed her cheek, and they went their separate ways.

CHAPTER 12

APRIL 21, 1900

Just after 1:00 p.m. on Saturday, Haydn and his friends gathered to watch the dedication of Galveston's new Texas Heroes Monument. They staked out a spot across from the platform where they could see the speakers and the monument.

At 1:30, a parade started. They watched a procession of school children, bands, public servants, civic societies, decorated wagons, and a display of "Red Men" and "Cowboys" that they whooped to as it passed. Haydn scanned the crowd until he spotted Rina.

She was on the other side of the street watching the procession with a friend, who he assumed was the Melanie she spoke of all the time. He stared at her, willing her to look at him, and as a group of letter carriers passed between them, he finally caught her eye. He smiled as large a smile as he could muster and raised his eyebrows in greeting. She smiled back with what seemed to be a look of relief, though he wasn't sure what she was relieved about.

At 4:00 p.m., Col. M.F. Mott introduced the various speakers on the platform, and the unveiling, prayers, speeches, and hymns followed. The program was finally brought to a close with a 17-gun salute to honor Texas Governor Joseph Draper Sayers, who was in attendance.

Haydn looked over the statue. It was a 72-foot structure honoring those who fought and died in the Battle of San Jacinto, a battle in the effort to win nationhood for the Republic of Texas from Mexico.

"It's certainly impressive," Haydn said. The monument stood at the intersection of Broadway and 25th Street and consisted of a 34-foot rectangular base, atop which rose four monolith columns. At the base of the columns, facing east and west, sat bronze statues of Defiance and Peace. Facing north and south were Sam Houston and Stephen F. Austin, heroes of Texas Independence. Atop the four columns was a 22-foot bronze statue of Victory, holding a laurel crown and gesturing toward the San Jacinto Battlefield, where another monument, aptly named the San Jacinto Monument, honored the same heroes as Galveston's monument.

"I think what's impressive is that they had the gumption to point it there," said Billingsley.

"They couldn't have done it intentionally," said Haydn.

"Even if they knew, what could they have done?" asked Peter. "They can't do anything about what lies between here and the battlefield."

"But she's pointing to Post Office Street!" Will laughed uproariously. "Isn't that fantastic? Victory is pointing to the red-light district!"

Peter punched him in the side. "Keep it down, you idiot!" he hissed. "My parents are somewhere close by."

Will continued to laugh, but lowered his voice. "Really, it is the funniest thing I've seen in a long time."

"You must not have looked in a mirror recently then," Haydn said to the hoots of his friends. "Well, it's been grand, but I think I've had enough of all this pomp, and besides, I prefer not to be seen with you reprobates."

"That's unfair. Will's the only reprobate," Billingsley said.

"Lay down with dogs," said Will, unfazed.

"On that note, I'll see you fellows later," Haydn said.

* * *

George looked out the window of a small apartment,

chewing his fingernails. He finally spotted Beatrice, and his stomach jumped. He watched her take a deep breath, look around, then push through the first-floor door to the building.

He heard her climb up the stairs to the second floor and proceed down the hall. He turned to face the door to the apartment and smoothed his hair. When she turned the key in the lock, he put his hands behind his back. She entered the room, closed the door behind her, and stepped in only a foot or so.

"Thank you for coming," George said, "Would you like to sit down?"

"I don't think I'll be here long enough for that," Beatrice said. Her voice was steady, but George could see tension in her shoulders. She added, "I'm sorry. It's just that I don't have much time. I was able to slip away for a few moments after the memorial ceremony, but I have to get back. We have plans."

George didn't ask for clarification who "we" meant.

"I understand," George said.

They both stood for a moment, facing each other, but not moving or speaking, then Beatrice said. "So, what do you want, George? As I said, I'll be missed."

"I know you will. That's what I wanted to talk to you about." George began to pace around the room. "Last night, my mother came home from the theater and told me she heard rumors that you and Lloyd will be announcing that you're engaged. Is that true?"

Beatrice didn't answer.

"You can't be serious, Bea."

She looked at the floor.

"He's not right for you," George said, taking a tone of a parent reasoning with an impulsive child. "He has no sense of humor. He has no panache. He's a nice enough fellow as those Midwestern types go, but good Lord, Bea, you'll be bored out of your mind within six months."

"There are worse things than boredom," Beatrice said, raising her chin and looking knowingly at George. His didactic veneer fractured. Emotion seeped through the cracks, melting the set of his face. His voice became a plea.

"You can't be in love with him, Bea."

Again, Beatrice didn't answer. She dropped her eyes.

"I knew it. You don't love him, do you? You still love me, don't you?" He started toward her, holding his hands out to grasp hers. When she took a step back and returned her gaze to the floor, he stopped.

"Bea, you're not denying it. I know you still love me. Why are you doing this?"

"You know why."

"No, I don't."

"Yes, you do!" she yelled.

George was surprised by her anger, but then her face softened. "George, I will always love you. You are a part of me, entwined through my heart like a vine. I couldn't remove you if I tried, which God knows I have. But I can't live with you, George. I can't live with your demons. They're destroying you, and if I let them, they'll destroy me, too."

"No, that's not true. Bea, you could help me. If I were with you, I wouldn't need to drink or gamble or any of that. I would be different."

"No, you wouldn't," she said, shaking her head. "I've been with you before, and you didn't stop."

"But I wasn't married to you, then. That would be different."

"You're right. It would. You'd be drowning right in front of me, and I'd try everything in my power to save you, and you'd pull us both under. There'd be nothing left alive inside of me by the time you were done with me, George. You'd break me."

George was devastated. "How can you say that, Bea? I'd never hurt you. I'm not like Adam Patterson. And you're certainly no Getrude Martin."

"No, you'd never beat me with your fists. I know that. But you'd beat the will out of me just as surely. Look where we are, George—a secret room having a secret meeting I can't tell Lloyd about. Secrets and lies and manipulations. You hate your life, your world, yourself. Everything about you is other than what it seems. I can't live like that. Maybe I don't love Lloyd as I've understood it with you. But I love his honesty, his stability, his openness. I love how simple everything is with him. And some day, maybe I will love him the way he loves me."

George made no effort to turn away as tears fell from his eyes and dropped to the floor. Beatrice lurched forward, and for a moment, George thought she was going to come to him, but she stopped herself and gripped her purse with both hands. Her knuckles turned white, and her face twisted with emotion. She looked up at the ceiling, took several breaths, then looked back at him, her face becoming a mask of composure.

"I won't come again, George," she said. She reached into her purse and placed her key on a table just inside the door. "I wish you peace, my love. Wish me happiness."

* * *

Haydn went to the beach and stood by a vendor selling flavored shaved ice. After a few minutes, he saw Rina walking toward him. She broke into a run the last few steps.

"I thought that ceremony would never be over!" she said, throwing her arms around his neck.

"Well, someone is happy to see me," he said. She removed her arms, and he stepped over toward the vendor cart.

"Of course I am," Rina said, her cheeks coloring.

"Though I admit, I might be a little happier than usual to see you today."

"Why?"

"To be honest, I was a little concerned you might not want to see me," she said, as Haydn bought them both cups of ice.

"What are you talking about?" he said, handing her a cup. They started walking.

"My behavior last night," she said. "I'm afraid I wasn't very ladylike."

"And I wasn't very gentleman-like, so I suppose that makes us perfect for one another," he said.

"You won't hold it against me, then?" Rina asked.

"Dear girl, I love you," Haydn said. "The only thing I could ever hold against you is if you did not love me back."

Rina dropped her cup of ice on the ground and again threw her arms around Haydn's neck. "You need never worry about that!"

A quick movement across the street caught Haydn's eye. A woman had come out of an apartment building across the street running. She held a handkerchief to her face, but Haydn recognized her.

"Wait here a moment," he said and pulled himself from Rina's embrace. He jogged across the street and cupped his hand around his mouth to shout out Beatrice's name when he saw George emerge from the building. Haydn stopped in the street.

George's head jerked in each direction until he spotted Beatrice. He looked as if he was about to run after her, but instead, he stayed where he was, watched her for a moment, then disappeared back inside the building.

Haydn looked up at the name carved into the building. Gulfview Terrace.

I remember that name from something, he thought. But he couldn't remember where. He motioned for Rina to stay where she was and followed George into the building.

He saw George disappear up the stairs. He climbed the steps to the second floor and looked down the hall. He watched George let himself into one of the apartments and eased his way down the hall until he was standing in front of the apartment. The door was slightly ajar, so Haydn peeked through the crack left by the door. He could see George sitting in a chair, his head in his hands. He pushed through the door.

"George?"

George raised his head, and tears stained his face. Haydn was paralyzed by the sight. He'd never seen George cry in his entire life, and he could neither move nor speak.

"Christ," George said, and his head dropped again, but this time his hands hung loose in front of him. He wiped his face with his palms and sat up straight. "What can I do for you, little brother?"

For a moment, Haydn couldn't speak, then he said, "I saw Beatrice."

"Ah, I see," George said wearily and stood up. "And now you're here, so you want to know what this place is and why Beatrice just left here like her hair was on fire. Is that it?"

"Yes, that would be it."

"Let's take the easy question first," George said. "This is an apartment I keep. I keep it so that I have a place to go when I can't stand prying eyes or ears."

It occurred to Haydn where he'd seen the name of these apartments. He'd seen it in the ledgers of his father's accounts that George managed.

"Does Father know you have it?"

"No, he doesn't, and I'd prefer it stayed that way."

"Fine with me, but what difference does it make? You're not in knee britches. If you want to keep an apartment, you can keep one."

"I have my reasons," George said. He moved toward Haydn and picked up the key Beatrice had left on the table next to the door. "Let's try this another way." He pressed the key into Haydn's hand.

"I just came into possession of an extra key," he said with a tight grin that disappeared as quickly as it had appeared. "The previous owner won't be needing it anymore, so now it's yours. If you'll keep quiet about this place, you may use it anytime you like, unless of course I'm here. But I don't imagine I'll be spending much time here for a while."

Haydn looked down at the key. Before he could say anything, George walked past him and out into the hall. Haydn heard George's footsteps descend the stairs, and then he was gone. Haydn looked around the room for a moment, then remembered Rina standing outside waiting for him, and he left, locking the door behind him.

CHAPTER 13

MAY 18, 1900

Margaret stood in front of a blank canvas in her third floor studio, unblinking and chewing on the handle of a paintbrush. Starting a new painting was always the hardest part—not only the actual act of painting, such as deciding where on the canvas to start, what colors, etc., but also deciding on a subject.

It seemed like she had lots of ideas when she was in the middle of another painting, trying to stay focused and follow a work through to completion. But when it was time to start something new, the universe of choices left her immobilized.

While she didn't like anyone telling her what to do, she also felt overwhelmed sometimes if she didn't have a particular direction in which to move. And so she stood, waiting for the muse to tell her what to do.

She heard the front door bell ring, then footsteps on the stairs, and a soft knock on the studio door. She grunted a muffled, "Yes?" and Sallie popped her head in the room.

"You have a caller, miss," Sallie said.

Margaret was relieved to have a reason to walk away from the empty canvas and pulled off her smock.

When she descended to the foyer, she was surprised to see Peter Martin.

"Peter?"

"Hello, Margaret," he said and bowed slightly.

"Were you looking for Haydn? I think Sallie may have misunderstood."

"No, she got it right. I'm here to see you."

"Oh," Margaret said and reflexively smoothed her skirt. "Well, what can I help you with?"

"Well, I've been thinking about you ever since I saw you at the Mardi Gras Ball, and I thought maybe it was time to do something about that," he said. "I'd like to court you."

Margaret felt her eyes widen. She'd had gentlemen callers before, but never one of Haydn's friends, and Peter's directness took her by surprise. But she realized that she quite liked directness, and a smile spread across her face.

"I see," she said. "In that case, how about we go to the parlor and sit? I'll have Elinor bring us some tea."

* * *

In the second floor apartment at Gulfview Terrace, Haydn and Rina sat across from one another, playing cards on the coffee table. Rina watched as Haydn took a card, pulled another one from his hand and put it face down on the table, then placed his hand on the table, fanned out and facing up.

"How do you like that?" he asked, triumph in his voice.

"I don't like it at all," Rina said, throwing down her cards. "It's not much fun playing games if I never win."

Haydn came around the table and sat next to her on the couch. He put his arms around her. She felt irritated and tried to pull away, but he held tight.

"You'll get the hang of it," he said. "And you win all the time with me, just not at cards."

"Do I?" she said.

"You won my heart without even trying," he said and kissed her neck. This made her giggle and she felt her frustration at the cards melt away.

"You're a smooth one," Rina said, smiling. They started to kiss, and after a few passionate moments, he lay down on top of her. Since they had started meeting at the apartment, neither of them pulled away anymore when things got physical.

Rina knew she shouldn't allow things to go as far as they did, but she got caught up in the excitement and just couldn't bring herself to stop. Honestly, she didn't want to. Each time, things went a little further, and with each new threshold crossed, she would feel a moment of panic, and they would stop. But then the next time, she looked forward to that kiss, that touch, that intake of breath. It was exhilarating.

She was sure she would never again feel this way about anyone. No matter what happened for the rest of her life, this would surely be the most exciting, most wonderful, most rapturous time of her entire life. And she didn't want it to stop.

Besides, he had told her that he loved her, hadn't he? He had said it a number of times, and she was sure he meant it. She meant it, too, when she said it. So, how wrong could all this really be?

No, she wasn't suddenly a debutante. She hadn't become a suitable society wife for Haydn in the last few months. And he hadn't mentioned marriage. None of that had changed. But, oh my, when he touched her.

"Would you be more comfortable on the bed?" he asked her, his voice hoarse.

Gasp! That lovely rush of adrenaline—there it was. She hesitated, then said, "I think I would."

* * *

George entered the small shop, and a man sitting behind the counter looked up and smiled.

"Mr. Winters, lovely to see you again."

"I'm sure," George said. He did not smile back.

"So, what treasures do you have for me today?"

George pulled a silver pocket watch on a chain out of his pocket and placed it on the counter. The man stood up, picked up the watch and inspected it.

"Very nice," he said. He placed the watch under the counter and pulled some bills out of his till. He handed them to George.

"That's all?" George said, looking from the bills to the man and back at the bills again. He felt certain that the more items he brought in, the less he was getting on each pawn.

"I'd say it's quite generous," the man said. "It's more than you had when you came in here, isn't it? And you're certainly welcome to come back and claim the watch. Just pay that back with the usual interest, and it'll be all yours again." The man pulled a cigar from his pocket and chewed on its end without lighting it.

"It's just that I need a little more than this. Is this the best you can do?"

"On that watch it is," he said, using the cigar to point

at the watch. "But I'm sure you can find some other items to make up the difference if you really need it." He sat back down, picked up a newspaper and started reading.

George looked once more at the cash in his hand then pocketed it and left the store. He pulled a flask from his pocket and took a long swig from it while mentally inventorying items in the house that might fetch a fair value but not be missed. He had run out of items that would be worth even bringing in. He had to find some cash.

CHAPTER 14

JUNE 17, 1900

Rina caressed the soft, white silk of the wedding dress. She had worked on many wedding dresses in her job at Mrs. Heckmann's shop, but this one was different. This one was personal. She held it up against her chest and looked in the mirror.

"Getting ideas?" Melanie asked, coming into the room.

"It's just beautiful," Rina replied, hanging the dress on a hook. "Are you getting excited?"

"I've been excited since the day John proposed," Melanie said. "Now, I'm just ready to get on with it!"

"I can't believe that in just a few weeks, you're going to be a married woman."

"I know," Melanie said. "I have to admit, I'm a little nervous."

"About what? You're not having second thoughts are you?"

"Bite your tongue," Melanie said. "No, I can't imagine loving anyone more than John, and I'm not nervous in the least about marrying him. I'm just a little nervous about what's supposed to happen after the wedding."

Rina was puzzled. "The reception? It's going to be lovely."

"No, you goose. After the reception—you know, when we're alone." Melanie raised her eyebrows at Rina.

"Oh, after, after," Rina said and nodded. "So you two have never…tested the waters?"

"Of course not," Melanie said. "I mean, we've kissed, and sometimes his hands have wandered a bit, but I told him that he wasn't marrying some girl from Post Office Street. He was going to make things legal if he wanted to go any further."

Rina felt her face flush. A girl from Post Office Street—is that what she'd become? "Of course," she said. She felt a little sick.

"What if it hurts?" Melanie said, dropping her voice almost to a whisper. "Or I don't like it?"

"I'm sure you'll figure it out," Rina said, turning her back to Melanie and picking imaginary lint from the wedding dress.

"I suppose," Melanie said.

Rina realized she didn't sound very supportive. Melanie was clearly scared about what to expect. While Rina knew information that might help her best friend prepare for the moment, she certainly couldn't tell Melanie that she had personal experience. Not after that Post Office Street remark. But she felt like she wasn't being a good friend letting Melanie worry without saying more. She sat on the couch and took Melanie's hand.

"It won't be that bad," Rina said. "I promise. Why, if it were something awful, women wouldn't do it, would they? And then there wouldn't be any babies. And there are an awful lot of babies around. So, there must be plenty of women that like it just fine."

Melanie smiled. "Well, that's true. There are a lot of babies."

"Yes, there are," Rina smiled back. "But you know what I really want to know?"

"What?"

"What are you going to wear on your honeymoon?"

"Oh, let me show you the clothes I've bought," Melanie said, jumping up and running over to the closet.

* * *

Haydn sat down at the dining room table. "I'm

starved. Can we just start, or do we have to wait for George?"

"We'll be waiting all day if we do that," Margaret said.

"We all eat together," Mildred said sternly, and Haydn and Margaret slumped in their seats.

"I'd like to eat this meal for lunch, not supper," Joseph said. "We're not waiting." Mildred started to protest, but Joseph picked up his fork and began to eat. Haydn and Margaret did the same.

"This family is losing all couth," Mildred said.

"Don't blame me for what George does," Margaret said, stuffing a bite into her mouth.

"Everything that everyone in this family does reflects on all the rest of us," Mildred said. "We are a family, and we each carry the family name. If one person sullies it, we are all sullied. I don't understand why that is so hard to grasp."

Haydn felt protective of George, knowing that he had been hurting deeply since Beatrice announced her engagement to Lloyd Preston.

"George isn't sullying the family name," he said. "He's just having a hard time right now. I'm sure it will pass."

"And what kind of damage will be done before it does?" Mildred said. "He's been gallivanting all over this town, staying out all night, doing god knows what with the worst kind of women. I can hardly hold my head up at card parties with the way he's carrying on. I'm sick with the thought that he's going to bring one of those women to our home."

"He's not going to bring a prostitute to the house," Haydn said, rolling his eyes.

"Of course he won't!" Mildred said, her eyes flashing. "That's not the kind of woman I was talking about."

"What were you talking about then?" Joseph asked, his attention momentarily drawn from his meal.

"Common girls, not prostitutes," Mildred said slowly, as if explaining something very basic to a child. "I've heard he's been escorting all sorts of girls around. If he shows up at this house with some nanny or shop girl, she'll rue the day she ever stepped foot across our threshold."

Haydn almost choked on the bite of food in his mouth. He took several sips of water to push the food down, then set his napkin on the table. Rue the day she ever stepped foot in the house?

He'd known his mother wouldn't be happy if he married Rina, but he'd started hoping over the last couple of months that he might be able to somehow get Mildred to accept her. He was more sure with each passing day that marrying Rina was what he wanted to do.

But he had no intention of bringing her into a home

where his mother would make it her mission to make Rina miserable. That would be cruel. And Mildred was making it perfectly clear that's what she would do to a girl like Rina.

They could just get their own home on the Island, but he didn't think that would be enough. If they lived on the Island, they would still be within Mildred's reach. No. He understood now that if he was going to marry Rina, they would have to leave Galveston.

Rina had said she didn't think she could leave Galveston, but he would just have to figure that out. He would be leaving for Virginia to go to school in the fall. Maybe he could have Rina join him there, and they'd marry without telling Mildred. Then they could bring Rina's father and grandmother to live with them there. Yes, that might work.

He wasn't sure if Rina would agree to the plan. He hadn't even discussed marriage with her yet. But he would remedy that—as soon as he was sure he had a workable plan for managing the issue with his family.

"I think that's enough for me," he said, pushing his chair back. He needed to go somewhere and think.

"I thought you said you were starving," Margaret said.

"I guess I wasn't as hungry as I thought."

CHAPTER 15

JULY 28, 1900

July felt like a Roman bath to Margaret.

"I don't know how you stand it up here," Emma said, fanning herself and leaning on a settee. The two girls were in Margaret's studio, and Margaret wished she could take off her paint smock, or the dress underneath, and get some relief from the heat.

While the studio, which was on the third floor of the Winters mansion, had windows on all sides, meaning it provided the best light in the house and was the best place to catch a breeze, the ceiling was not elevated. So it felt as if it were pressing hot air down on them, like a clothes press for humans.

"Just try not to think about it," Margaret said, trying

to take her own advice and ignore the sweat trickling down her side.

"That's like not thinking about breathing when you're under water," Emma said.

Margaret ignored her and focused on the canvas in front of her. The image that stared back at her was one of her favorites: Bettie Brown, a personal hero. Miss Bettie, as everyone called her, was a 45-year-old socialite spitfire that Margaret modeled herself after.

Aside from being a Brown, which made Miss Bettie a member of one of the most prominent families in Galveston, she was also unmarried, a painter, and fiercely independent. Bettie had traveled the world, had studied art, and, best of all in Margaret's eyes, she did exactly as she pleased, whether Galveston liked it or not. One time, Margaret saw her racing her carriage unchaperoned down Broadway. Oh, how Margaret wanted to do that!

"Your mother is going to have a fit if she sees that," Emma said.

Aside from the fact that Mildred wouldn't like Margaret idolizing a woman like Bettie Brown, refined women weren't supposed to paint original subjects. They were only supposed to copy works by others. Margaret didn't much care whether she was supposed to paint Bettie Brown or not. She was going to do it. But thinking of Mildred reminded Margaret about the only aspect of Bettie that Margaret did not wish to emulate—her bouts of melancholy.

Like Mildred, Bettie sometimes wrestled with periods of deep sadness. Such things weren't discussed openly in polite society, but under their breaths, people discussed the details, real or imagined, about Bettie's "visits" out of town for "rest." Margaret knew this meant people also whispered about Mildred's visits out of town for the same reason.

Margaret felt a pang of sympathy for her mother. The idea that one's personal demons were discussed at card parties made her sick. Yet she knew she did the same thing when it was someone else's demons, and it was she playing cards. All the same, her mother's pain, or hers, was no one else's business. She just wished things worked that way.

"I know," Margaret said. She didn't want to talk about her mother, though. She changed the subject. "You know, I'm seeing Peter today. He's going to be here any minute."

"Are you now?" Emma said, sitting up. "It sounds like you two might be getting serious."

"Well, I'll admit that he's proven to be quite the entertaining companion," Margaret said. She was beginning to think that it might not be so bad to have a partner with her as she travelled the world and raced carriages, and she thought that perhaps she could do worse than Peter Martin. "Marriage doesn't seem quite as unpleasant as it used to."

"Marriage!" Emma said, clasping her hands together. "Oh, my God, did I just hear Margaret Winters say she's getting married?"

"No, you did not," Margaret said, putting her hands on her hips. "I just said that it doesn't seem as...confining as it once did. I'm not necessarily sold on the idea, but let's just say I'm enjoying Peter's efforts to sell me. If that's what he's doing. He hasn't mentioned it, and neither have I. So don't go blabbing that to anyone!"

"My lips are sealed," Emma said, pursing her lips together.

A bell rang out through the house.

"That's him," Margaret said. "I'm late." She pulled a sheet down over the painting and took off her smock. She primped and smoothed her hair in a mirror, drying her sweaty face with a clean edge of the smock, then turned to Emma.

"How do I look?"

"Like a woman who might be getting married," Emma said.

Margaret picked up a paint brush and threw it at Emma.

Emma laughed, and the two girls headed downstairs.

When they got to the foyer, she said goodbye to Emma and went to the parlor where Peter was waiting for her.

"Hello, Peter, how are you today?"

Peter rose from where he had been sitting and bowed slightly.

"Hello Margaret. You look lovely as always."

"You're very sweet."

"Where's your mother?" he asked. For the few months that he'd been courting Margaret, they had met in the parlor once a week. They played cards or listened to the phonograph or just talked. At first, Mrs. Winters sat in the corner of the room, doing needlework and pretending not to listen to their conversation, while she did exactly that.

But Mrs. Winters had either decided that Peter was harmless or, more likely, she wanted to increase the pace of his and Margaret's courtship, because recently she had not chaperoned them after greeting him on his arrival. And today, she hadn't even bothered to greet him at the door.

"I guess she had something more important to do today than make sure I didn't embarrass the family with improper or immodest behavior while entertaining a gentleman."

"Never," Peter said and lowered his eyebrows. He then smiled and asked her, "Was there something special you wanted to do today?"

"Why don't we go for a walk?" she suggested. "I've been cooped up in this house all day, and I could use a little fresh air. How about a stroll on the beach?"

"All right. But instead of a stroll, why don't we ride? I've got my carriage with me."

"Even better," she said.

Without telling her mother where they were going, Margaret strode out the front door. Peter trailed behind, looking to see if Mrs. Winters would appear so he could tell her where they were going. No one appeared, so he followed Margaret out the door.

The breeze by the shore made the weather much more comfortable than it had been in the attic studio, and Margaret enjoyed the ride. As they passed by a long pier that reached out across the water, she got a sly grin and asked Peter, "Do you ever go on night swims?"

She could see him trying not to act shocked that she'd asked. She knew he was getting to know her well enough by now to expect anything, but she could still surprise him. Instead of answering her question, though, he responded with a question of his own.

"Have you?"

"Once," she said.

Peter's mouth fell open, and Margaret laughed.

"You...you've swum at night...without clothes...off the pier, under the electric lights?" Peter asked.

"No one can see anything if you swim out a bit from the pier or stay close to the shore," she said. "My girlfriends said I wouldn't do it, and you know me. I couldn't let a challenge like that go unanswered. So, we snuck out to the beach one night, and I...well, I just did it. I shimmied right out of my dress and plunged into the water. It was exhilarating!"

The look of shock on Peter's face started to make her feel uneasy. Normally, she enjoyed making a man squirm, but as she told the story, she found herself worrying that perhaps she'd gone too far. She liked the idea of keeping Peter on his toes, but in an unusual twist for her, she realized she didn't want to drive him away.

"I didn't jump from the pier in the light, you understand. No one saw anything," she added quickly. "I'm not even sure my friends could see me, with it being at night and all."

Peter's look of surprise began to morph into a smile.

"So, what did your friends think?"

Margaret felt a wave of relief. He was smiling!

"They were mortified, of course! I thought they both might faint right there on the beach. It was fantastic!"

Peter laughed and took her hand. They looked around, still laughing, and saw Haydn coming out of an apartment building. Margaret raised her hand to call out to him but stopped herself. A young woman had walked out of the building with him. She walked in the opposite direction, but she looked back at Haydn, who glanced over his shoulder and blew the woman a kiss. The woman giggled and walked on. Margaret and Peter both stared at her until she disappeared around a corner.

"Do you know that girl?" Margaret asked.

"No, I don't," Peter said. "Do you?"

"I've never seen her in my life. What is she doing with Haydn?"

"That's a good question."

CHAPTER 16

JULY 28, 1900

Haydn sat at a table in the Martin family's drawing room, looking intently at a handful of cards. A breeze pushed through an open window, but did little to relieve the heat in the room, and he sat with the collar on his shirt loosened and sleeves pushed up.

"How is it still so hot, even at night?" he asked.

"Summer," Will said. "What else is new?"

"Speaking of summer, Winters, how goes yours?" Peter asked. "We never see hide nor hair of you anymore."

"You see me all the time," Haydn said.

"For cards, but when was the last time we men just sat around and said what was on our minds?" Peter said.

"What are you, Martin—a woman?" Will asked, laying a card down on the table and signaling Billingsley for another.

"He does have some nice curls in his hair," Haydn said.

"You wish you had this hair," Peter said, running his left hand through his hair. "I just wondered what's been eating up your attention lately."

"You're one to talk," Edward said. "Since you've been seeing Margaret, we've had to hire private detectives to see if you've left town."

"Margaret?" Haydn asked. "Margaret who?"

"Very funny," Edward said.

"What's funny?" Haydn said.

"My God, I think he's serious," Will said, setting his cards face down on the table. "Are you serious?"

Haydn looked at him blankly, and Will's mouth dropped open. "Winters, you idiot, he's dating your sister. Do you not live at home anymore?"

"My sister?" Haydn said, surprised.

"Is there a problem with that?" Peter asked evenly.

"Well, no. I guess," Haydn said, shrugging. "I mean, I don't know. How long has this been going on?"

"It's been almost three months, Hy," Edward said. "You astound me."

"I've just been preoccupied, I guess," Haydn said. "I really don't know how I feel about this Peter. You know she doesn't want to get married, so what exactly are your intentions?"

"My intentions are to court her, out in the open, until she agrees to marry me," Peter said, looking at his cards. He then looked Haydn in the eye, "You can relate, right? Or maybe you can't. You don't have any philosophical objections to openly courting someone do you? Is there someone you're concealing from us?"

Haydn froze. "What do you mean?"

"He doesn't understand you when you use big words like 'philosophical objections'," Will said.

Billingsley laughed. "Yes, let's take a simpler approach." He leaned in and looked closely at Haydn's face. Haydn pulled back. "Nope," Billingsley announced. "No ring through his nose, so no woman in his life."

"Is that so?" Peter said.

Peter looked back at his cards, and Haydn studied him, then stood up.

"I could use a break," Haydn said, stretching his arms up. "Peter, show me what beers you've got in the kitchen."

Will pushed his chair back and stretched his legs out. "Suddenly need a beer break, eh? I'll bet I can guess who didn't have a good hand."

"Peter, the beer?" Haydn said, ignoring Will.

"Sure," Peter said, and stood up.

When they got to the kitchen, Haydn asked Peter,

"What was that about?"

"What do you mean?" Peter said innocently.

"You know what I mean. What were you trying to get at?"

Peter took a breath, then said, "I saw you coming out of an apartment building down by the beach today, and I saw that you were there with a woman."

Haydn started to protest, but Peter went on.

"Light brown hair, nice face, petite."

Haydn pursed his lips. Peter continued.

"It's obvious you don't want anyone to know about whatever it is you're doing with this girl, since you're denying that you're even seeing anyone, but you're not being very careful. If you're trying to have some kind of clandestine tryst, you need to work on the clandestine part. Margaret and I both saw you."

"Margaret knows?" Haydn said.

"She was right there with me," Peter said. "She saw the whole thing."

"Well, it's not some tryst," Haydn said. "The girl you saw—she's not some cheap tart. She's special. I love her."

It was the first time Haydn had said those words to anyone except Rina, and the emotion of hearing the words out loud made his chest feel full.

"I love her," he said again. "I know it looks bad, and you're right. I should have already told my family...and my friends. I just wanted some time and some privacy to figure out what we were, and what we can be, without anyone's interference. Can you understand that?"

"Do you mean your mother?" Peter asked.

Haydn nodded.

"Then yes, I can understand. She can be a real bear, can't she?"

"You have no idea," Haydn said.

"Well, I won't say anything. And I'll talk to Margaret. I can't guarantee she won't say anything, but I'll do what I can." Haydn gave Peter a grateful smile.

"Thank you. I would appreciate that."

* * *

Mildred sat listening to music on the phonograph and holding a cup of tea. She didn't hear the music, though, and her tea had long gone cold. She was engrossed in thought, and when she slipped into the deep recesses of her mind, little stimuli from the outside could penetrate her consciousness.

When she first sat down, her thoughts had been on Margaret. She was sure that Peter Martin would propose soon, and she prayed Margaret would accept. A union between the Winters and the Martins would be monumental in terms of society. But Margaret was an unpredictable girl. If she thought Mildred wanted the marriage, Margaret might rebuff the Martin boy out of pure spite.

On the other hand, Margaret seemed to have genuinely fallen for the young man. If she really did want him, perhaps she might, for once, allow Mildred to guide her. Heaven knew Margaret had no experience in keeping a suitor. She had actively worked until now to avoid attracting one. It was a miracle Peter Martin had even tried.

In fact, Mildred was sure Margaret would mess things up, and she couldn't let that happen. She had to help Margaret.

She set the teacup down and started pacing.

The girl was unlikely to help herself, and Mildred had to make sure that at least one of her children married well. The boys didn't seem to be too interested in doing so.

George had come so close with Beatrice. For the life of her, Mildred couldn't understand what had happened between him and Beatrice. And he wasn't likely to ever tell her. They hadn't had a heart-to-heart conversation since George was a boy.

There was a time the two of them had been close. There was a time she and Joseph had been close, too. Or at least, she'd imagined that they were. She looked at her wedding ring and felt a phantom of remembered sentiment.

She had loved Joseph passionately when they

married. Her father, George Painter, had been unsure of Joseph's motives when Joseph had started courting her. He had expressed concern that the young man seemed a bit driven. He worried that possibly Joseph wanted entrée into Mildred's social world and his business world more than he actually wanted Mildred. Mildred had cried bitterly when her father said this to her. Mr. Painter could not stand to see his daughter cry and promised he would take the young man under his wing. He did, to Mildred's delight, and a wedding soon followed.

Mildred picked up the framed wedding photo of her and Joseph that sat on the shelf among books and trinkets. She thought about how their marriage was in those early years. She was supportive and encouraging. Joseph quickly mastered the ins and outs of banking and finance. He was a gifted young man, and Mildred was proud to be his wife.

When little George was born, she had been thrilled, and her father had been touched that she named the little boy after him. She remembered the severe bout of melancholy that she suffered for a time immediate following the boy's birth, and she felt ashamed. How could she have felt anything but joy about him? But when the darkness lifted, she had become a warm, loving mother, hadn't she? She adored her first born.

As the years had gone by, though, and Joseph's successes had mounted, Joseph no longer paid her much attention. He no longer sought her counsel or discussed business with her. It seemed he no longer needed the caché of being her husband as he became known for his own business acumen. She was no longer needed, and therefore, she felt she was no longer particularly wanted. She set the wedding photo back on the shelf, and tears welled in her eyes.

Elinor opened the door to the study. "I'm done in the kitchen, ma'am, unless you need something else."

"All I need is privacy," Mildred said sharply, turning her face away so Elinor wouldn't see her tears.

"Yes, ma'am," Elinor said and shut the door.

Mildred wiped the tears away. She had never confided in anyone how terribly hurt she was by her husband's tacit rejection. Her pride had made her unable to admit that she may have made a mistake, so she directed her pain in the only direction she could—inward. She decided that if she didn't let anyone get close to her, they couldn't hurt her.

When her father slumped to the floor one day with a heart attack, making Joseph the chief executive of Mr. Painter's business interests, Mildred felt that the last remaining gentle piece of her soul died with him. She spent a month "resting" out of town after his death, and when she returned, Joseph had moved the family into Painter House.

Mr. Painter had left his assets to Mildred's mother,

but as the male head of the household, Joseph took control and managed the family finances. He argued persuasively that the family could best look after Mrs. Painter by living with her. With his installment in the mansion, the transition of Joseph from protégé to captain of industry was complete.

Mildred felt used and bitter, and she vowed her own children would never be swindled the way she felt she had been. She had told George from an early age that the family business would be his someday—that he was the rightful heir. She made sure he knew that it was her father, not his, who had started the family fortune, and she let him know that it would be his to steer someday. When that day came, and George took the helm, she would finally feel that a piece of her and her father were back in charge.

But lately George had begun to worry her. Something was wrong, and Mildred feared the decline she'd seen in him lately. He was rarely home, and when he was, he was drunk. He had lost weight and seemed distracted and even slightly disheveled much of the time. He seemed angry, or maybe it was sad. She didn't know what it was exactly.

She just knew that the light that characterized her older son seemed to be dimming. Something in him was fading away. And as it did, she felt something of her own future, her own self, dying with it.

Overflow

She felt powerless to stop it. And she didn't like feeling powerless.

CHAPTER 17

JULY 29, 1900

Haydn kissed Rina passionately on the couch in George's beachfront apartment. He moved to lay her down, but she resisted, pulling away and moving a few inches away from him. She needed to talk to him, and she was determined not to get sidetracked.

"Aren't you going to ask me about the wedding last night?" she asked.

"Of course," he said. "It's been the only thing on my mind."

"I can tell," she said, slapping him playfully on the arm. "Well, since you care so much, it was wonderful. Melanie and John were made for each other, and the ceremony couldn't have been more beautiful."

Rina described the flowers and dresses and the reception, but she didn't tell him about her many dances with Frederick. She wasn't sure if Haydn would be jealous, but she knew there was no reason to be, so why upset him? Besides, she already had something to tell him that might upset him, and it was far bigger than a few dances with Frederick. She chose her battles.

"I love you," she said.

"I love you, too," he said and moved to kiss her again. She stood up.

"I mean that I really love you," she said. "I wouldn't do anything to hurt you or to try to force you to do something you don't want to do."

"I know that, silly bird!"

"Good. I'm glad that you know I would never manipulate you," she said and started to pace. "Because sometimes things happen, and things change, and there was no intention to change anything, but it just happens. Do you know what I mean?"

"I think I know what you're getting at," Haydn said. "It's Melanie's wedding isn't it? It must have stirred a number of feelings for you. And I don't want you to worry. Because I have every intention of making things right between us."

Rina felt a flutter in her stomach and stopped pacing. "You do?"

"Yes. I found out last night that Peter and Margaret

know about us, so it may be time to change things for us."

"How do they know?" Rina asked.

"They saw us leaving the apartment yesterday. I don't know if Margaret knew exactly what's going on, but Peter certainly did. He says he won't say anything, but there's no guarantee that Margaret won't get a bee in her bonnet and spout something out to my parents. So, maybe we should…well, Rina would you—"

The front door slammed open, and Haydn and Rina jumped. George looked at the two of them, and said, "Hy? What are you doing here?" His tongue was thick and his words were slurred.

Haydn touched Rina's shoulder. "Rina, would you wait for me in the bedroom? I need to talk to my brother for a moment."

When she was gone, Haydn asked George, "What's going on? You don't look well."

"That's because I'm not. I'm not well in any sense of the word. I'm a goddam mess, in fact."

Haydn had never heard George talk like this, and he was unsure what to say. So, he put his hand on George's shoulder. "Is there anything I can do for you?"

George looked up at him, and tears welled in his eyes.

"Who is she?" George asked, jutting his chin toward the bedroom and wiping away his tears.

"Someone I've known for a little while," Haydn said.

"Do I know her?"

"No," Haydn said, shaking his head. "We've been keeping things quiet."

"For how long?"

Haydn shrugged. "About five months."

"Five months?" George said, opening his eyes wider. "Well, someone's gotten good at keeping a secret. This is serious, isn't it? I can see it on your face. Does Mother know?"

"That didn't seem wise," Haydn said. He glanced toward the bedroom. "I think it may be time, though, to get things out in the open."

"Are you sure?" George asked, lowering his voice. "You know Mother won't approve. If she were someone Mother would approve of, I'd know her."

Haydn shifted his weight. "Well, Mother is going to have to get used to it, because I'm going to ask her to marry me, and I don't care if you think I'm crazy or Mother doesn't like it or anything else. I love her."

George thought for a moment then nodded his head.

"Then marry her," he said. "Stay away from Post Office Street and bourbon and gambling and Mother and marry the girl."

Haydn didn't have those vices, and George knew that, but now didn't seem to be the moment to correct him.

"Leave the bank," George continued. "You don't like it there. In fact, leave Galveston. Make a life for yourself with this woman doing something you like. Write stories or help minister to animals or whatever it is that makes you happy. Forgive me for not being entirely sure what that is. It seems there's a great deal I don't know about you these days, and it's not your fault. It's mine. I'm a terrible brother."

"That's not true!"

George waved him off and continued.

"I don't know what it is that you want to do, but I know that it's not counting bills," George said. "You do a good job, and you come to work every day like you're supposed to, and customers like you, but you don't really like it, Hy. Anyone can see that. And you wouldn't like being an attorney any more than you like being a bank teller. Learn from my mistakes, little brother. Don't let Mother and Father plot your life for you." He met Haydn's gaze. "You want to do something for me? Live your own life. That's what you can do."

Haydn wanted to say something, but he was at an utter loss for words. So instead, he stepped to the bedroom and motioned for Rina to come out.

"Rina, there's someone I'd like you to meet." He put his arm around her waist. "This is my brother George."

"It's a pleasure to meet you," Rina said, bowing her head slightly.

"It's a pleasure to meet you, too, Rina," George said. He bent to take her hand to kiss it, but he lost his balance and landed on the couch.

Haydn walked her to the door. "I'd like to stay with my brother for a while, but will you come back here tomorrow afternoon, during your lunch break? There's something I'd like to ask you, but now is not the time."

"Of course," she said. She kissed him quickly, and Haydn shut the door.

* * *

A little while later, George let himself into the bank and sat down at his desk. Haydn had offered to talk things through with him at the apartment, but George told him he needed some time to himself to figure some things out. He'd sent Haydn on his way, and he had planned on just staying at the apartment, but once he was alone, he found he didn't want to be there.

He reached into his desk drawer and took out a bottle. He poured himself a drink and chuckled to himself. So, Haydn was having a secret affair. He would never have guessed his younger brother had it in him to pull off such subterfuge. And to defy their mother by courting someone who was clearly not among their circle? He had underestimated his younger brother.

George had tried, in his way, to stand up to Mildred

and Joseph, but he had made a mess of it. When he first started gambling, it wasn't for the money or even the sport. It was a statement. It was a way of taking control of something. He couldn't control the outcome of the events he wagered on, but the rest of the process was within his control. He decided what to wager on, how much, how often. He watched odds change and calculated his bets. It was an exercise in decision-making and choice. It was all in his hands.

He wasn't entirely sure when the sand beneath him had begun to shift. When had it become something that controlled him instead of the other way around? He didn't know. But when he finally realized that it had become one more force outside of himself, pushing his life into decisions he didn't want to make, actions he didn't want to take, he felt an overwhelming despair.

He drained the glass and sat it on the desk. He stared at the glass. That's really when he had begun drinking more, wasn't it? He hadn't wanted to think. He had just wanted to be numb. But that, too, had slipped out of his control. Everything he came in contact with overtook him, and he was losing the few things he cared about.

Beatrice was gone, engaged to marry that Lloyd weasel, and now, here he was, risking the one thing left he wanted to preserve—his job at the bank. He threw the glass on the floor, but it refused to break. He put his head in his hands.

For a long time, he believed that he didn't really want to be his father's protégé, that he didn't want to be molded into the company's future. But that wasn't true.

George enjoyed working at the bank. He liked going to business lunches and meeting other men of business and learning about the other aspects of his father's business dealings. He had ideas about the future of the business, and he actually looked forward to someday taking over the whole empire. He believed he was good at it.

He just resented that he was never given a choice about the matter. No one had ever asked him if he wanted to take over the company someday. His mother had never once asked him about his interests or encouraged him in any hobbies. Mildred and Joseph had both always spoken as if it were a known fact that George would succeed his father in the business, and that was that.

He knew that this was expected of most first-born sons. He wasn't under the illusion that his situation was unique. But knowing that didn't change how he felt, which was that no one seemed to care what he was feeling or what he wanted. His life was planned before he was out of knee britches, and it had been his role simply to fulfill the destiny laid out for him without asking questions or expressing opinions.

He got up and walked to the vault and spun the dial

with the combination. He pulled the heavy door open and stepped inside.

He looked at the cash all around and asked himself if he could really do this again. He had done this twice before without getting caught. *If you tempt fate often enough*, he heard his father's voice in his head, *eventually it will bite you*.

Hearing his father's voice in his ears, the familiar resentment welled in his chest, and he grabbed the money he needed from a shelf in front of him.

"This is the last time," George said aloud. "I mean it. The last time."

There's always a next time. The words of Reynolds' henchman rang in his ears.

"Everyone, just shut up!" he screamed to the empty room.

He stepped into the dim lobby of the bank, shoved the door to the vault shut, and strode to his desk. He threw the money onto his desk, sat down in his chair, and pulled out an apartment house ledger.

For the second time that day, his eyes filled with tears. He didn't bother to wipe his eyes this time. He just began making adjustments to the numbers in the ledger. When he was done, he emptied the bottle on his desk, and watched the room become darker and darker, until he could see nothing in front of him anymore.

CHAPTER 18

JULY 29, 1900

Rina knocked on Melanie's door fast and hard. When Melanie answered, she looked slightly alarmed.

"Rina! My word, is something wrong? You were banging like the house was on fire!"

"No, nothing is wrong. Something is very, very right!"

Melanie ushered her into the small house she and John were renting. John's belongings were everywhere in boxes. He had begun moving them into the house a week ago. Melanie's possessions, including a trunk packed for her honeymoon, were still at her parents' house, but Melanie was here to oversee the delivery of furniture. Tomorrow morning, the Klaussens would take Melanie and John to the docks to leave on a four-week honeymoon to Germany, and Rina was anxious to talk to Melanie before they left.

"What's going on?" Melanie asked.

"Is John here?" Rina looked around.

"No," Melanie said. "But he'll be back in just a few minutes."

"Well then I'd better hurry," Rina said. "I have so much to tell you, but I want to tell you alone."

"What has gotten in to you? I've never seen you so—"

"I'm going to be married!" Rina blurted out.

"What? Married? Did Frederick propose again? Last night at the wedding?"

"It's not Frederick, Melanie."

"Not Frederick?" Melanie's brow knitted. "Who else could it be?"

"His name is Haydn, and he's wonderful," Rina began to flit around the room. "He's handsome and kind and gentle and smart, and we're going to be married."

Melanie's mouth fell open, but no sound came out. Rina continued to talk in a rush, the words spilling out.

"He hasn't actually asked me yet, but he's going to tomorrow, and it's just in time."

"Just in time for what? And who is this boy?"

"Let me start at the beginning," Rina said. She told Melanie everything she'd been keeping from her since

February, and when she finished, Melanie looked stunned.

"You're sure he's going to propose tomorrow?" Melanie asked.

"I'm sure," Rina said, smiling.

"Rina, do you have any idea how lucky you are? What if he didn't marry you?" Melanie still looked worried.

"I know. It could have all gone terribly wrong," Rina admitted. "I've made mistakes, I know, and I hope you won't think less of me. When this day started, I was terrified that I'd probably ruined my life. But tomorrow, he'll ask me to marry him, and it will all work out. Who knows? I may be married by the time you get back! That's why I just had to tell you before you left. I didn't want you to come home and be shocked!"

"Well, I am shocked! I wish you would've confided in me sooner, but I'm glad you told me now," she hugged Rina. "When I get home, we'll celebrate everything properly. I understand if you can't wait for me to come home to get married, but you are going to get a party when I get home, do you hear me?"

Rina laughed. "Yes, ma'am," she said.

The front door opened, and John shoved a large trunk into the foyer of the small house.

"I'm home, wife!" he shouted.

"Wife. Isn't that wonderful?" Melanie grinned at

Rina. John stepped into the front room where the two women were sitting.

"Rina, how nice to see you," he looked at her and narrowed his eyes. "You look like a cat with a bird stashed somewhere," he said. The two women giggled.

"Something like that," Rina said.

"Did you come to see us off?" John asked.

"She just wanted to make sure I was all caught up on gossip before we left," Melanie answered for her. "Three weeks is a long time. Who knows what news we'll come back to when we return, right, Rina?"

* * *

"Haydn, good to see you!" Peter said, clapping Haydn on the shoulder. "I've been wanting to talk to you, so I'm glad you could come by."

"Well, I wanted to talk to you, too," Haydn said. "I wanted you to be the first to know, since you already sort of do. I've decided to ask Rina to marry me."

"Really?" Peter asked, his face lighting up.

"Yes. I've known since I met her that I would some day, and thanks to you and Margaret so rudely sticking your nose into my affairs by taking carriage rides, the day has come."

"Don't blame me that you can't keep a secret," Peter joked.

"Seriously," Haydn said, "I'm going to ask her tomorrow. I was going to ask her today, but something came up, so I'm going to ask her tomorrow, then tell my family. I want it to already be decided before I say anything to my mother. She's not going to like it."

"Well, I may be able to help you with that aspect of things," Peter said.

"How do you mean?"

"I think I can give your mother something else to focus on. I've decided to propose to Margaret as well."

"That's wonderful!" Haydn said and embraced Peter.

"I thought that I'd come to your house tomorrow evening, after your father gets home, and ask him for her hand. If he approves—"

"I think you can count on that."

"Well, if he does, then I'll ask Margaret, and God willing, she won't make me suffer by refusing to answer right away. But I'm fully prepared to wait her out if she does!"

"By God, the girl has met her match," Haydn said. "You bring up a good point, though. I wonder if Rina will want me to ask her father for her hand?"

"Can you ask him first? Does he seem like a good sort?"

"I've never met him actually."

"Really?" Peter asked, and his tone made Haydn feel a little embarrassed.

"It's all been a bit untraditional," Haydn said. "I'm sure Rina and I can figure that part out." He felt stupid that he hadn't thought about that sooner and wanted to steer the conversation away from him and Rina. "I really am glad you're going to ask for Margaret's hand," he said. "And not just because it will distract Mother. You know, you might be getting more than you bargain for with my sister, but Margaret is certainly getting a top-notch man. I couldn't have chosen a better husband for her myself, or a better brother-in-law."

"Thank you, Haydn. That means a lot. I know you and Will have always been closer friends than you and I, but I think we'll make grand brothers-in-law!"

Haydn took his hand firmly. "Future husbands and brothers-in-law!"

* * *

Margaret dabbed paint onto the portrait in front of her. The sun had set and the gaslight in her studio was sufficient but not ideal, so she didn't plan to work much longer. She just wanted to put on a few finishing touches before calling it a night.

"How can you see in that dim light?" Mildred's voice interrupted.

Margaret jumped and turned. She stepped in front of the painting.

"Are you worried about my eyes or the painting?" she asked.

"Neither, actually," Mildred said, stepping into the room. "I want to talk to you about something. I've been waiting for you to come down, but it looks like you'll be up here all night, so Mohammed has come to the mountain."

"Oh, you're a prophet now, are you?"

Mildred held up her hand. "I'm not here to argue. I'm here to help."

Margaret cocked her head to the side. "Help? With what?"

"With Peter."

Margaret let out a laugh. "With Peter? I don't need any help with Peter."

"You may not think you do, but by the time you know that you do, it will be too late. I know you love the boy, and I want to make sure that you don't make a mess of things. This could end well for you if you'll just listen to a little advice."

"You don't give advice. You issue demands."

"I'm not here to demand anything," Mildred said. Her tone sounded so reasonable that Margaret was immediately suspicious. "I'm simply here to offer the benefit of experience. I've been watching things progress between you and Peter, and I daresay that a proposal is imminent. He's going to propose to you anytime now.

I'm sure of it. And I think we should talk about how you'll accept—what you should say and what needs to happen afterward. A wedding of this magnitude has to be handled just so."

"Oh, I see—how I'll accept. So, you think I don't even know how to say, 'No, thank you?'" Margaret didn't actually think that she would want to respond by turning down a proposal from Peter. In fact, she was sure she didn't, if a proposal actually was imminent. But she didn't like Mildred inserting herself into things, and if there was to be a wedding, she had no intention of letting Mildred commandeer it. The shocked look on Mildred's face was satisfying.

"You'll say no such thing!"

"Don't tell me what to say," Margaret said, her voice rising. She turned her back to Mildred and jerked a sheet down over her painting.

"You're acting like a child," Mildred said. "I know you want to marry the boy. Any fool could see that. So this is nothing more than an attempt to put a stick in my eye. And it's ridiculous. Now, let's talk about this sensibly."

"There's nothing to talk about, Mother. I never said I'm marrying Peter, and I never said I'm not. But whatever I do, you'll have to look elsewhere for your society wedding. If you want a wedding with the Martins so badly, perhaps you can convince George to marry

Peter's sister Gertrude if she ever leaves that beast of a husband of hers, provided he doesn't beat her to death first. Throw them a wedding. The damsel in distress and her knight in shining armor."

Mildred stood in silence for several seconds, her mouth open, while Margaret took off her paint smock and straightened her supplies.

"Adam Patterson beats Gertrude?"

"Oh, please," Margaret said. "Don't pretend you don't know."

"I had no idea."

Margaret crossed her arms and looked at her mother for a long moment.

"You really didn't know?" Margaret asked. Mildred dropped her head. Margaret softened. "Mother, he hits her. Often. That's why she lost her baby."

"How do you know this?"

"Everyone knows. The whole town knows."

"I never heard that!" Mildred said, her head snapping up, and Margaret could see in her eyes that the revelation—either that Getrude was abused or that Mildred had not been privy to the gossip about it—hurt her. Margaret felt a wave of sympathy for Mildred. She really didn't have much in her life besides all this society drivel, did she?

"Well, Peter confirmed it," Margaret said. "He said Adam got drunk one night, something he does most nights, and on this night, something upset him. Who knows what it was. Peter said it could have been how far open the windows were or what dress Gertrude wore that day. It never takes much. But he hit her. She fell, and he started kicking her. It was too much for the baby."

Mildred instinctively put her hands to her stomach. "I never heard any of that," Mildred said.

"I'm sure Mrs. Martin doesn't talk about it," Margaret said. A moment passed, and Mildred stiffened.

"Yes, well, that would hardly be appropriate conversation," Mildred said. "In fact, no one should be talking about it. Families should keep their dirty laundry to themselves. You'll be part of that family soon, so you shouldn't go around spreading gossip like that. It's unseemly."

Margaret narrowed her eyes. Well, that little moment of weakness hadn't lasted long, had it? She couldn't believe she had actually felt sorry for Mildred.

"Family is overrated," she said. "So, you can talk George into rescuing Gertrude when Adam is done with her. Or maybe Haydn. That can be your lavish Martin wedding. Just don't look to me to provide it for you."

She pushed past Mildred and stomped down the stairs.

CHAPTER 19

JULY 29, 1900

Haydn eased through the front door. He and Peter had gone out to celebrate, and he didn't want to wake up the household. He closed the door behind him, hearing it click into place, and walked gingerly toward the stairs. As he passed the parlor, his father's voice drifted flatly to his ears.

"Haydn? Come here please."

Haydn jumped, then peered into the parlor. The room was dark, and he could barely make out the outline of his father, sitting back in a chair, legs crossed, facing the foyer. He smelled cigar smoke and thought how angry his mother would be that his father was smoking cigars in the room where she took callers.

He stepped into the parlor doorway, blocking what little light filtered in from the hall. The grandfather clock by the front door began to chime 11:00 p.m. The two men waited for the chimes to stop, and then Haydn spoke.

"I'm sorry I'm coming in so late. I'll be on time to the bank tomorrow. I promise."

"George is dead."

Haydn stood, paralyzed. He could not have heard what he just thought he did. He and Peter had drunk quite a bit of celebratory beer. His mind must be muddled.

"I'm sorry, father, what did you say?"

"You'll have to open the bank tomorrow morning. I need to make arrangements with Mr. Levy, the undertaker. He has George's...body," he cleared his throat, paused for a beat, then continued. "But there are decisions to make. Many decisions." Joseph looked Haydn in the eye, and the realization came over Haydn that his father hadn't already been looking at him. He had been looking past, or more accurately, through Haydn up to that point. "I can count on you to handle the bank, can't I?"

"Of course," Haydn managed to say through a strangled throat. He could barely think, and breathing had become difficult. His head was swimming. This wasn't happening. It couldn't be.

"Father, what happened?" His voice came out as a whisper. Joseph's gaze returned to its previous empty focus.

"He fell."

"Fell? What do you mean? Fell from where?"

"He was on the stairs, and he lost his footing. He fell." Joseph's voice betrayed no emotion.

"How? When?"

"I don't wish to discuss this any further, so go to bed. Tomorrow will be a long day."

Haydn hesitated, then turned and walked to the foot of the stairs. He looked up the expanse of steps, no more murderous in appearance than they had been this morning. But he didn't want to touch them. He knew he must climb them if he didn't want to keep standing where he was, with his father behind him, staring he was sure, but he couldn't lift his foot to the first stair. His head began to swim, and he felt his legs going soft beneath him. He grabbed the banister to steady himself.

Gripping the banister with all his might, he took a deep breath, put his foot on the first step and pushed his body up. He had a vision of George splayed in front of him, and he wondered if he was stepping on the last place his brother had drawn breath.

A visceral grief seeped into his rib cage, and a lump in his throat became painful. His eyes began to burn with tears he didn't want to shed in front of his father. He didn't want to climb these damn steps! He felt sick. But there was no other way to the second floor, to get to his bedroom where he could cry in peace. He had to climb these stairs.

So, he took another deep breath, pressed himself against the banister, and propelled himself up each step, until he reached the top. Once there, he heard a muffled sob float up from the parlor. Haydn realized he'd been holding his breath, and he let it go, immediately sucking in more air with a sob of his own and lunged for his bedroom.

Haydn lay down on his bed on top of the sheets, fully clothed, and cried in the dark as the clock next to his bed ticked loudly. He wondered why time hadn't stopped. Time should've stopped. How could seconds continue to tick by when George was dead? He needed everything to just stop for a moment so he could grasp what had happened, what was happening. What exactly was he supposed to do tomorrow? What was his role, his duty? He was to open the bank, but what else?

He didn't want tomorrow to come. That there would even be a tomorrow without George was unfathomable. He just needed everything to stop. He heard the clock in the hall chime at 15 minutes past the hour, and he buried his face in his pillow.

CHAPTER 20

JULY 30, 1900

Haydn awoke the next morning, groggy from fitful and inadequate sleep. When he finally drifted off, he dreamed vivid and intense dreams, which slipped away from him as consciousness overtook him. His head ached, and his eyes burned.

As he remembered the events of last night, he wanted to cry but was too spent to muster the energy. He was emotionally drained. And as he remembered his father's directive to open the bank, the exhaustion became physical. He wasn't sure he could move. But he had to. So he lifted off his bedsheet, damp with sweat, and swung his legs over the side of the bed.

At some point in the night, he must have removed

his clothes, because he wasn't wearing them now, but he didn't remember taking them off.

When he appeared downstairs, dressed for work, he found the house unusually quiet. While he had no interest in speaking to anyone, he found it strange there was no sound of voices anywhere, nor footsteps or the sound of anyone moving around. He pushed open the door to the dining room and saw the table clean of dishes. He entered the kitchen and found Jefferson and Elinor sitting silently at a table. Elinor sniffled and Jefferson held her hand.

"Where is everyone?" Haydn asked.

"Gone," Elinor said, and tears began to fall down her cheeks in worn paths.

"Mr. Winters went to talk to Mr. Levi about preparations, and Ma'am and Miss Margaret have left," Jefferson answered.

"Left?" Haydn was bewildered. "Left where? What about the funeral?"

At the mention of the funeral, a strangled noise escaped from Elinor's throat. Jefferson patted her hand, then looked back at Haydn. "They wasn't in no condition to go to a funeral, Mr. Haydn."

"I don't understand," Haydn said. "They're not coming to the funeral? Either of them?"

"The sight of Mr. George—it was too much," Jefferson said.

"They saw him? They saw him fall?"

"I don't think we should be talking about this," Elinor said.

"Mr. Haydn, nobody told us nothing about when they'd be back, but I don't think either one is going to be back for the service," Jefferson said. "You is all Mr. Joseph got at the moment."

Haydn felt a weight land on his shoulders, like something massive was pressing him into the ground. He could barely stand. He was being thrust into a role he wasn't prepared for. He and his father barely spoke, and he was supposed to be some kind of pillar for him to lean on?

No, Jefferson had it wrong. His father didn't need to lean on him. His father didn't need anything from him other than for him to open the bank, which he would go do right now.

He pushed through the kitchen door then stopped just inside the dining room, trying to remember where he'd put his keys. Through the kitchen door he heard Elinor say, "That boy don't understand the storm brewin' around him."

* * *

Haydn turned the key in the lock of the bank's front doors and opened them. He wasn't used to arriving at the bank when it was empty. His father or George always got there first. George. Haydn felt tears start to well again, but he brushed them roughly away.

He looked at George's desk. A ledger was open on the desk. *This must be the last thing George worked on*, Haydn thought, his throat constricted. He walked over and put his fingers on the open page, as if by touching the book George had touched, he could touch George.

His emotions threatened him again, and he started to close the book so he could put it away when he noticed the entries in the ledger. They were receipts from the apartment building where George kept the clandestine apartment. The entries were messy. He had clearly erased and revised the receipt amounts several times.

Haydn saw that George had written in a tenant name for the clandestine apartment. Haydn knew there was no such tenant, and he looked at the fake name for several seconds, wondering where he'd come up with it. Was it from a book? Was it someone George knew? He'd never even bothered to ask George how he maintained the apartment without their father knowing. Now, he suddenly had millions of questions for George— questions that would never be answered.

The front door opened, and Stefan entered the quiet bank. He gave Haydn a pained look and opened his arms. Haydn wondered how he already knew. Had Joseph called him, unconvinced that Haydn would do as he asked?

It didn't matter. Haydn walked over to him, tears filling his eyes, and collapsed against Stefan's chest. Stefan held him tightly without saying a word, and Haydn heaved tears onto the older man's waistcoat. He felt like a child, and with a child's fears, he was terrified that his family would collapse under the weight of George's loss, and he would be left alone to bear his grief and the obligations of his family's future.

When Haydn calmed down and wiped his face, he straightened. "I need to prepare the bank for the day's business," he told Stefan. "I promised Father."

"We will do this together," Stefan said.

Haydn found as he moved through the morning routine that he knew more than he thought he did about what to do. But when he was unsure, Stefan was able to fill in the gaps in his knowledge.

"I don't know what I would've done if I'd had to do all this by myself," Haydn said to Stefan.

"You knew most of what to do," Stefan waved off the gratitude.

"That's not what I mean. I probably could've figured out the steps to take, but I'm not sure I would've had the strength to take them without you here."

"I will always be here for you, my boy," Stefan squeezed Haydn's shoulder.

Haydn looked at the old man and felt a wave of warmth. He felt his eyes starting to well again with tears.

Stefan took a somber tone.

"There will be much for you to take on now. Do you understand that?"

Haydn didn't want to understand it, but he did.

"You will take George's place now," Stefan clarified.

"I know."

"Not just at the bank, my boy, but also as heir to the family," Stefan pressed on. "You are the only son now. Everything will fall to you. Your parents will expect you to learn the business, and take on the family's social and public obligations."

Haydn nodded.

"That means…" Stefan waited for Haydn to meet his eye, then continued "they'll expect you to marry according to an heir's position."

Haydn squeezed the bridge of his nose with his thumb and forefinger. Rina. He hadn't even thought about her yet and how all this would affect their plans. It was all happening too fast. There was too much to think about, too much to do.

"What will you do, Haydn, about the girl?" Stefan asked in a softer tone.

Haydn had not told Stefan that he planned to ask Rina to marry him today, but he knew that Stefan would know it was coming. He started to open his mouth, then closed it and raked his fingers through his hair. He bent over and put his hands on his knees. He stayed like that for several seconds, then he stood up again.

"I have to let her go, don't I?" Haydn asked.

Stefan didn't reply.

"It wouldn't be right to bring her into my life now, no matter what I want. My mother will never accept her. It was one thing when I was the 'extra' son. Mother wouldn't have liked it, but we could move away. I could start another life somewhere else, and George and Margaret could fulfill the social obligations of the family. Rina and I could have our own life somewhere else. But I have to stay now. I can't just do whatever I want. I have to help my family. And it wouldn't be fair to put that on Rina," Haydn said.

Haydn saw sadness on the old man's face, and he thought that Stefan was disappointed in him.

"You know what it would be like," Haydn said. "Mother would spend every waking moment letting Rina know that she wasn't good enough or trying to turn her into someone she's not. It would be misery for her, Stefan. I should know. All my life I've wanted out, and now I should ask the woman I love to endure what I never could? I can't ask that of her, Stefan. I can't do it. I want her to be happy, and she would never be if she married me now. I was born to this, but she wasn't. If I love her, I won't ask her to live this life with me."

Stefan took Haydn's face in his hands. "My boy, you must do what you feel is right. It is not for anyone to question or judge it." Then he put a hand on Haydn's heart. "Do what you feel is right."

CHAPTER 21

JULY 30, 1900

Haydn entered the beach apartment, shut the door and sat in a chair, staring at the floor.

A few seconds later, he heard a knock at the door. He answered the door, and before he could say anything, Rina threw her arms around his neck.

"I thought lunch would never get here!" she said.

Haydn pulled loose and took a few steps into the room, keeping his face turned away from Rina. This was going to be harder than he'd imagined.

"I need to talk to you," he said quietly.

"Good! I need to talk to you, too. But you go first," she said. He turned around and looked at her.

"I think you should probably sit," he said, gesturing

toward the couch. She took a good look at his face, and her smile faded. Without saying anything, she sat on the edge of the couch cushion.

"What is it?" she asked. Her voice was neutral, but Haydn could see that she knew something was wrong, and he couldn't look at her. He looked at the floor a few feet in front of her.

"I can't…see you anymore."

When she didn't respond, he looked up to meet her gaze. Her mouth hung open in shock, and he looked away again quickly.

After what felt like an eternity, she closed her mouth, sat straighter and said, "I see."

Her hands were clasped in her lap, and the knuckles had turned white.

"There's been an accident," Haydn said. "George is dead."

"Oh my god!" Rina jumped up from the cushion and rushed over to Haydn with her arms out, but when she got to him, he stepped back before she could embrace him. She stopped short and her arms fell awkwardly to her sides.

"This changes things, Rina." He looked into her eyes, pleading with her to understand, but what he saw was confusion, sympathy and the edges of what seemed to be panic.

"I'm so sorry," he said turning away. "I never

dreamed anything like this would happen. I can barely grasp it myself. The last 12 hours have been a blur."

Rina had gone pale and looked like she might lose her balance. Haydn stepped toward her and eased her back onto the couch. "I don't understand," she finally managed. "I'm sorry for your loss, of course, but I don't understand what this has to do with us."

"I'm so sorry, Rina. I don't understand it all myself yet, except that I know that the right thing to do is to let you go. My life is not going to be what I thought it was going to be. Everything is different now. I don't have the freedom that I had this time yesterday. I don't have the choices—not in my work, not in my life. Not in marriage. It's not what I want, but I have obligations now."

"We all do," she said, an edge creeping into her voice.

"You don't understand," Haydn shook his head. "My family is going to need me. I can no longer just think about what I want. I have to think about what they need. I have to find out what my father wants me to do about school and what kind of obligation this will present for me regarding my mother and sister. I'm the eldest son now. I was never prepared for this, Rina. I don't know what it all means."

"I don't understand where this sudden feeling of family loyalty comes from," Rina said. Her breaths were coming harder, and when she looked at Haydn, her eyes flashed with anger.

"I don't know," Haydn said, caught off guard. "I guess I've never been needed before. It was easy to talk about leaving and doing whatever I wanted when it didn't matter to anyone. But what I do actually matters now."

"Yes," she said, her voice hard. "It certainly does."

Her tone threw him off balance. He had expected tears…maybe hysterics. But Rina wasn't crying. And she wasn't hysterical. She was angry. And he didn't know how to respond.

"You don't understand the position I'm in," he said, his voice trailing off.

"Oh, but I do," said. "It's you who doesn't understand my position. But that's not really your concern anymore, is it?" She stood up. "You're George now, and George would never marry someone like me, would he? He would never lower himself to marry some seamstress, would he?" She was gesturing, and her voice had grown loud.

"Rina, I—"

"Enough!" she shouted. "I've heard enough. I've heard more than enough. I don't care to hear another word about your obligations and your sense of duty." She said the last three words with such derision that Haydn simply looked at the floor.

Rina stomped away from him, jerked the door to the apartment open and slammed it behind her.

Overflow

Haydn sat down in the chair she had vacated. He leaned over, and his head fell into his hands. He felt nauseated, and he began to cry.

* * *

Rina ran out into the sunlight. Tears were streaming down her face, and she squinted against the glare from the sand street.

She stumbled around the corner of the building and collapsed against the wall. She held her abdomen and cried openly.

"Ma'am, are you all right?" A washerwoman set down a basket of clothes and touched her shoulder. Rina continued to cry for a few more seconds, then took a deep breath.

"I will be," she said wiped her face with her skirts. "I just lost something, that's all."

"Do you want some help to find it?" the woman asked.

"Thank you, no." Rina attempted a grateful smile. "I'll get another one. It won't be the same, but no one will ever know it's not the right one."

"Just you, honey." The woman smiled, patted her shoulder, then picked up the basket of dirty laundry and continued up the street.

Rina watched the woman until she turned a corner.

Overflow

Then she stood up, brushed off her dress, smoothed her hair and walked back to work.

CHAPTER 22

AUGUST 28, 1900

The August heat pressed through Haydn's clothes, and he felt a film of sweat cover his body. Since George's accident, the heat had intensified with each passing day, and Haydn was less able to cool off at the beach or escape the stifling bank than he used to be. His responsibilities to the family and the business took up most of his time.

He sat at George's desk—he still thought of it as George's—and worked on ledgers. It was tedious work, and he had already been through them once, but he was double-checking his work, partly because he liked to be sure it was right, and partly to keep his mind occupied. When he was busy, he didn't think of Rina.

George was harder to push out of his mind, though. Reminders of him were everywhere. Not only did he use his brother's desk all day, but many of the documents and ledgers he dealt with were written in George's hand.

Joseph set some papers on the desk and said, "Don't forget we have lunch with some gentleman from the cotton exchange today. We'll need to leave in about an hour."

Haydn sighed. He hated all the business lunches Joseph insisted Haydn attend with him. Aside from being bored senseless by the conversation, on each and every outing someone expressed a condolence about George. He kept hoping that would stop soon, and clearly Joseph felt the same way, because he always just murmured a solemn, "Thank you," and immediately changed the subject.

Haydn had tried a few times to talk to Joseph about what had happened to George, but his father would just press his lips together, look intently at his newspaper or some bank document, and say, "The details are irrelevant."

The more Haydn had seen of George's papers, though, the more convinced he had become that the details were, in fact, relevant. Many of the documents showed numbers that had been worked and re-worked. At first, he thought his brother may have been having trouble keeping things straight because he was upset and distracted in his final weeks. But now he was beginning to think there might be a darker reason. Now he wondered if George was trying to hide something in the numbers.

He was sure that George had been in real trouble before his death. Anyone could have seen that he was drinking too much, and he was bordering on distraught when Haydn talked to him in the apartment before his death. But was George also in financial trouble?

If so, that made him think that the details surrounding George's death might, in fact, be very important. Maybe it wasn't just a tragic accident. Maybe George had purposely thrown himself down the stairs. He needed to know what really happened that night. But talking about George seemed only to shut Joseph down further.

So, he had changed tactics. He wasn't sure if the servants had been in the house that night, but maybe they had heard something, even if they hadn't seen anything. He had decided to try and find out what, if anything, they knew.

With only Haydn and his father taking up residence in the mansion, the Coles didn't have as much to do. But Haydn had seen Sallie dusting in Margaret's bedroom about a week ago and had tried to talk to her.

"Do you miss Margaret, Sallie?" he had asked her from the doorway.

"I certainly has less to do." She kept dusting.

Haydn had nodded, his hands in his pockets. The question had just been something to say. Margaret had never been particularly friendly to Sallie, so it didn't seem to break the ice much.

"We certainly all miss George," he tried again.

"Yes, we do," she said. Her voice was sad, and he felt like he had an opening.

"Were you home when it happened?" He moved into the room. He reached out a hand to pat her shoulder, but to his surprise, instead of accepting his sympathy, she looked up at him with what could only be interpreted as fear in her eyes.

"I don't know nothin', Mr. Haydn," she had said, shaking her head vigorously. "And I got chores to do downstairs." She had rushed past him before he could say another word.

Haydn had stared after her. Sitting at his desk now, he thought about the exchange, and he was sure that the suspicions that had lurked in his mind since he'd taken over for George at the bank were right. There was more to George's death than a simple fall. He was sure of it. And Sallie knew something about it.

He tried a couple more times to talk to her, but after that day, she had avoided him...or at least he thought she did. Maybe it was his imagination. Maybe his suspicions, too, were just his imagination. Maybe he was the one who should have gone for a "rest." He shook his head. No, there was something going on.

He was glad that Margaret and his mother were coming home today. Well, that wasn't true. He was glad Margaret was coming home. He didn't want to be alone with Joseph anymore, and Margaret would lighten things up. For all her faults, Margaret would not mope around. She wasn't the moping type. And maybe she would tell him what his father wouldn't—what exactly had happened the night George died.

He knew Peter would be happy to have her home as well. George's accident happened before Peter had the chance to propose to her, and Peter had been patient, but Haydn knew he was eager to ask for her hand.

He'd like to say he was happy about his mother coming home, too, but he couldn't honestly say that. But again, maybe with her home, things would return to some sense of normalcy…or at least, as normal as things would ever be again.

The door to the bank opened and Haydn looked up.

"Well, if it isn't Galveston's newest captain of industry!" Will boomed.

"What are you doing here, you sorry excuse?" Haydn smiled.

"Sorry excuse for what?"

"I can't say. I'm a gentleman."

"Not true," Will said. He shook Haydn's hand and deposited himself in the chair in front of Haydn's desk.

"Since I never hear from you anymore, I decided to come looking for you. I thought maybe you had jumped a steamer out of town."

"I wish I had," Haydn admitted.

"Well, I'm on the verge of getting offended, Hy," Will said only half-joking. "Since George died, you never come around. You haven't even been to the card games. Martin seems to be the only one who ever talks to you."

"I'm sorry," Haydn said. "I know I've been a bit underground. It's just been a difficult time. Peter only sees me because he comes by the house all the time looking for information on Margaret. Have we heard from her? When will she be back? He's really quite pathetic."

"Goes without saying," Will grinned for a moment, then dropped the smile. "Seriously, Hy, is everything all right?"

"I suppose," Haydn said, gesturing with his palms up. "I mean, I've taken over for George, and Mother and Margaret are coming home today, and I guess all the necessary things have been taken care of, but some things still aren't right."

"How about we talk about it tonight over some cards or a beer?"

"Tonight isn't good with Mother and Margaret coming home, but there's a boxing exhibition tomorrow. I could go to that."

"Perfect," Will said, slapping his thighs and standing up. "It's a date, then! Will you bring me flowers?"

"I'll bring you a kick in the pants."

"Good enough."

* * *

"So, it would appear that I can't leave you alone for five minutes without a circus breaking out," Melanie said, settling herself on a worn couch.

"Five minutes would have been fine, but if you leave for weeks at a time, I have to do something to entertain myself while you jaunt around the world on history's longest honeymoon," Rina said with a wry expression. She was so glad that Melanie was home and she finally had someone to talk to. The month since Melanie had left, since she and Haydn had split up, had been one of the hardest of her life. She had never felt so alone.

"Not true," Melanie shook her head. "Some rich people honeymoon for a year or more. I barely got started by that standard."

"Oh well, then," Rina said.

"Seriously, Rina, what happened?" Melanie asked, all joking gone from her voice. "I'm not so terribly shocked that I came home to find you married. I'm just shocked at who you're married to. What happened with Haydn?"

Rina's smile faded. "He broke things off."

"That cad," Melanie said, her hands balled into fists in her lap.

"It's not as bad as it sounds," Rina said. "He didn't know about the baby."

"What then? And why didn't you tell him?"

"I didn't have the chance," Rina stood and started to pace. "I was going to tell him. I had my words all ready. But before I could say any of them, he told me his brother had died and everything had changed and he couldn't marry me. And that was that."

"So, you didn't tell him? Maybe if you had told him, that wouldn't have been that."

"You weren't there," Rina said defensively. "And I wasn't going to beg."

"So, you went to Frederick and told him you would marry him," Melanie said, no trace of judgment in her voice.

"Yes. And last night, I told him that I'm pregnant. He's thrilled," Rina said.

"Of course he is," Melanie said, trying to smile a reassuring smile. She then asked hesitantly, "What about you, Rina? How do you feel?"

"I feel lucky," Rina said, lifting her chin. "Frederick is a good man. He will treat me well and love our baby, and we'll have a good life together. It could have been so much worse." They were the right words, and they were true enough, but Rina left out the part where she'd cried herself to sleep every night for the first two weeks after Haydn had dismissed her. If Melanie had been here when it happened, she would have told her everything. But now, she felt like it was important to look forward, not backward. There was nothing she could do now about the past, and reliving it was only going to cause her more pain.

"But you still love Haydn?" Melanie's face showed compassion, and Rina felt her face flush.

"I will always love Haydn," she said. Saying the words sent a knife through her chest. She rested her hand on her stomach, and for a moment, she wanted to hash through all of her conflicted feelings with Melanie—her feelings for Haydn, the feelings she wished she had for Frederick, her fears about how she could raise this baby and not look at him or her every day and think about Haydn, her guilt about lying to her family.

But before the feelings could overwhelm her, she took a deep breath, willed her mind to quiet, and said, "But that was all just a dream. I should've known that from the start. Men like Haydn don't marry girls like me. I made a foolish mistake, and God has blessed me with a way to make it right. I'm very lucky," she said and nodded her head as if to drive home the point.

Melanie got up from the couch and put her arms around Rina. After a moment, she released her and said, "So, show me where the nursery will be!"

"You're sitting in it," Rina laughed. "There's not much room in this house. I'm grateful to Frederick's parents for letting us live with them until we can move to our own apartment, but we're really tripping over one another. Tell your father to pay my husband more!"

"Consider it done," Melanie laughed.

"Good. Now tell me every single detail about your honeymoon!" Rina said.

CHAPTER 23

AUGUST 28, 1900

Margaret stared out of the carriage window at the front of the house, where her father was waiting for her and Mildred. When the carriage pulled to a stop, Joseph helped them both from the cab, and Jefferson unloaded their luggage.

Mildred entered the front door and walked directly upstairs, but Margaret paused. She stood in the open door and stared at the staircase.

"Come along, pet," Joseph said and squeezed her shoulder. Tears almost sprang to her eyes. Her father hadn't used an endearment with her for as long as she could remember. When she was a child, he called her "pet" so often that she thought it was a real name. She was so confused when children at school began to talk about their pets. She thought for a long time that it meant they all had little sisters at home.

When she revealed this to a group of boys and girls one day, one of the boys pointed at her and laughed. He corrected her mistake, but not before the other children's peels of laughter had caused Margaret's face to go red with embarrassment and anger. It was this face that had greeted Joseph when he came home from the bank that night.

Margaret had demanded, arms folded defiantly across her chest, to know why her father would call her an animal. Mystified, Joseph had asked his little girl what she was going on about. When she told him, he was unable to suppress a grin. Margaret, indignant, stamped out the room.

George found her later in the sun porch, crying. He explained that calling her "pet" was Joseph's way of telling her he loved her. She didn't believe him at first, but eventually George convinced her.

Margaret smiled and was about to remind Joseph about the incident, then decided that perhaps it wasn't the time for revisiting the past, recent or distant. Now was the time to move forward. That's what the doctor at the resort had told her. The past could not be changed, and while Margaret would never forget George's accident, she must soldier on. Otherwise, she might end up like her mother, battling melancholy for the rest of her life. And that, she was resolute, she would not do.

So, she took a deep breath, lifted her skirts and marched into the house.

* * *

An hour or so later, Sallie was helping Margaret unpack when they both heard the front door bell.

"Miss Margaret, you have a caller," Jefferson called up the stairs.

She walked down the stairs, focusing on the handrail instead of the steps.

"I'm so glad you're home! The world can start spinning again," Peter's voice floated up to her.

She looked down at his smiling face and felt a wave of relief and pleasure. She'd been strong until this moment, but seeing Peter, she felt raw emotion stick in her throat. She almost couldn't think of a smart retort—almost.

"Have I been gone long?" she asked.

"An eternity," he said, taking her hands when she reached the bottom step. He kissed her on the cheek and lingered for a moment with his face near hers.

"So, tell me," she said, forcing composure. "What has gone on while I was gone? It must have been terribly boring."

"Terribly," said Peter.

"I'm sorry I haven't written," Margaret said, and she meant it.

"Well, I admit, I was a little worried that maybe you'd forgotten me, or run away with someone," Peter said. Margaret could tell he was only partly joking.

"Never," Margaret said. "I've gotten you all broken in, just how I want you. I couldn't possibly start over with someone new." In her month away at the spa, she had had a lot of time to think—about George's accident, the future, what really mattered. And she had realized some things.

She loved her freedom, and her painting, and she still did not want to live her mother's life. But she also wasn't willing to give up happiness in the service of defiance. She loved Peter. That was certain. And he didn't seem to have any interest in changing her into her mother, or his. So resisting marriage to spite her mother or because she feared something that really didn't appear to be an issue was just folly. It was immature. And it was most certainly time to grow up.

She looked at Peter smiling at her and embraced him. When she released him, they walked into the parlor and sat down.

"Tell me about the funeral," she said to him, her voice low and serious.

"Are you sure?"

"Yes. I need to know about it."

Peter told her the details—where it was, who attended, who spoke, etc. Margaret asked questions here and there, but mostly just listened. Her eyes moistened with tears several times, but she pressed Peter's handkerchief to her eyes and motioned for him to continue.

"How was Beatrice?" she asked.

"Not well, I'm afraid," Peter said. "She cried continuously. Lloyd had to hold her up. It was uncomfortable to see her so distraught, especially in front of her husband, knowing her history with George, except that Lloyd was so understanding. Another man might have told her to get a hold of herself or walked away, humiliated, but not Lloyd.

"He kept his arm around her, kissed her temple and stroked her hair. And when she would start to sob at times, he would whisper in her ear. She was an open wound. You've never seen anyone in such pain."

Margaret thought about George's decline after Beatrice became engaged to Lloyd.

"Yes, I have," she said. "But I'm glad Lloyd treats her well. That would've meant a lot to George."

"Lloyd really loves her," Peter said. He squeezed her hand then sat up straighter and cleared his throat. "Speaking of men who love women, there's something I'd like to ask you."

"What about women who love men? Do they count for anything?" Margaret asked, arching an eyebrow.

"They're all that counts," he said.

"In that case, I love you, too," she said and gave his hand a squeeze in return.

"Well, that's good. It makes my question a bit easier." He dropped to one knee and held her hand. "Margaret, I shall never again, as long as I live, meet anyone like you. I shall never want to. And I shall never again want to be parted from you like this.

"You are all that I want, all that I need, and no substitute could ever fill the space that you now occupy in my heart. I am yours for the rest of time. The only question is if you will be mine. Margaret Winters, will you be my wife?"

"I wouldn't have it any other way," Margaret said and kissed him.

CHAPTER 24

AUGUST 29, 1900

"So, the fair Margaret has been captured, then?" Will asked with a grin. He and Haydn were walking home from the boxing exhibition.

"Like a wild lion," Haydn replied.

"God help Peter," Will laughed.

"True," Haydn said. "Though I must admit, and I acknowledge it may just be temporary, but I think she's actually been a bit more—what's the word?—tame, I'd say, since returning from her trip with my mother."

"I wouldn't let her hear you say that," Will said. He then took on a boxer's stance and pretended to throw punches at Haydn. "I'll show you 'tame'!" he screeched in a high-pitched voice.

Haydn laughed.

"You may think this sounds strange," Haydn began hesitantly, "but I think there may be a reason, besides Peter's velvet charms, that Margaret is more subdued."

"Can you bottle and sell the reason?"

"I'm serious," Haydn said.

"Sorry," Will said, cocking his head and looking at Haydn. "I see that you are. Go on, then."

"I think that Margaret may know something—something I suspect, but can't get anyone to confirm."

"What do you think she knows?" Will raised his eyebrows.

"What really happened to George."

"What do you mean 'what *really* happened'?" Will asked. "You know what happened to George."

"No, I know what my family tells me happened, or rather what my father told me the night George died," Haydn said. He picked up a rock from the road and threw it into the distance at nothing. "He's refused to talk about it since then, and my mother and Margaret haven't said a word about him since they came home. It's like there's some taboo about talking about him, which makes me wonder."

"Wonder what?" Will asked cautiously.

"It makes me wonder if there was something taboo about what happened."

"I don't know what you're saying, but I'm sure I

don't like it," Will said. He looked around the street, and Haydn guessed that he wanted to be sure no one was listening to their conversation.

"I don't like it myself," Haydn admitted. "But if I'm right, George deserves our compassion, not our shame."

"What exactly are you suggesting?" Will asked, his brow furrowed.

Haydn pulled at his earlobe, then finally let out a breath of air and said, "I think George killed himself."

As soon as the words were out of his mouth, Haydn felt sick. It was the first time he had said them out loud, and voicing them gave them a weight that Haydn hadn't expected. He felt heaviness settle on his shoulders and in his chest.

"What?" Will stopped walking. The two men looked at each other.

"I think he threw himself down the stairs," Haydn said.

"That's crazy, Hy." Will shook his head then started walking again, his steps faster and harder than before. "George wouldn't do that."

"I think he would," Haydn said, rushing to catch up to him. "You didn't see him just before he died. Things were really bad, Will, and he was in a real state. I'd never seen him like that before."

"No, no, no," Will said. "I saw him plenty of times, out and about, and he was his usual self, laughing and drinking and genial."

"Yes, you saw him drinking. Always drinking, wasn't he? Did you see him anytime in the last few months before his death when he wasn't drinking?"

Will slowed his pace but didn't answer.

"You don't know how it really was, Will. Nobody did," Haydn said, a pang of guilt punching his stomach. It was fine for Will to not see George's pain, but how could he have been so obtuse? "He was very adept at showing people only what he wanted them to see," he continued, trying to explain not only to Will, but to himself.

"But all that laughing and geniality...that wasn't real. Since I've taken over for him at the bank, I've found out just how bad things were. I've seen the books he was keeping for the bank, and Will, he had made a real mess of things. It's not just that, though.

"He tried to talk to me, just before the accident happened, and I think he was much worse off about Beatrice's marriage to Lloyd than any of us realized, too. All that drinking wasn't just George being frivolous or irresponsible or the life of the party. I think he was trying to drown something. I think he was distraught, Will. And not just about Beatrice. Like I said, he'd made a real mess of things."

"What kind of mess?" Will asked.

Haydn looked down then around at the darkened houses. He heard a dog bark, and through one of the open windows, a baby started to cry.

"I think he was in trouble from his gambling," Haydn said. "I think he was stealing."

"What?" Will exclaimed, then lowered his voice. "From whom?"

"The books he was keeping at the bank were laughable," Haydn said. "I've been going through his accounts, and amounts don't add up. And he had changed the numbers several times. I spent all afternoon yesterday looking at everything, and I can only come to one conclusion. I think he was stealing from the safe and trying to move the numbers around to hide it. I'm still trying to get everything in balance without Father knowing."

"Oh no," Will said.

"It gets worse. I found some money missing from my room, too. My mother said the other day that she thought the servants had been stealing. She said there were small, expensive items missing from all over the house. I didn't really think much of it at the time, but in light of what I found at the bank, I thought I should look into it.

"So when I got home last night, I searched his room, and I found a note. I call it a note, but I think it was actually some kind of tab—an ever-increasing tab. That's when I realized about the gambling. I'm sure he took all the things from the house and sold them. So, I checked my room. I keep some money in a drawer at home, and when I counted it, there was some missing."

"Are you sure it's not some kind of coincidence?" Will asked.

Haydn gave him a withering look.

"Well, then, is there any chance he had just gotten sloppy with his recordkeeping from the drinking?" Will asked.

"It wasn't accidental," Haydn said shaking his head. He started walking again. "He had purposely written inaccuracies in the ledgers. There were changes, over and over...as he stole."

Will chewed on his lower lip. Haydn could tell he was beginning to believe the same thing Haydn did. It was a relief to have someone in his confidence. He'd been bearing the burden alone since he began to realize the truth of the situation. He hadn't even told Stefan, in whom he could normally confide anything.

But Stefan loved George and wouldn't want to believe it, and if he did, he might feel obligated to tell Joseph that George had been stealing, and Haydn didn't want that. Haydn had to see if someone outside the family's inner circle would see what he was seeing. And for all Will's antics, he knew his best friend would keep the conversation private.

They reached Haydn's front gate and Will started to push through the gate, but Haydn stopped him.

"No, let's not go in yet," Haydn said. He closed the gate and lowered his voice. "Too many prying ears in there."

Will shut the gate.

"Think about it," Haydn continued "It would explain why Margaret went out of town with mother. She's never escorted her before. If Margaret knows how George died, then it makes sense that Father would want to get her out of town to calm down."

"Margaret's not really the hysterical type," Will said doubtfully.

"Not normally, I'll grant you, but something like this? I didn't see her before she left, but she must have been devastated," Haydn said. "And Father would have never trusted her discretion."

Will let out a heavy breath and ran his fingers through his hair. He looked up at the house. "Good God, Hy. What are you going to do?"

"I'm going to find out the truth, that's what."

"What good can that possibly do?" Will asked. "If it's true, you'll just ruin George's name—maybe the whole family's."

"I won't tell the whole island," Haydn reasoned. "I'll keep it in the family. But George deserves the truth."

"George knows the truth," Will said. "And I can't think that it matters much to him now."

"Well, he deserves for his family to face up to the

truth and to love him anyway," Haydn said, crossing his arms. "And Margaret deserves to be relieved of the yoke put around her neck keeping the secret. She's starting a new life. She shouldn't have to do it weighed down by a secret."

"I just don't know what good you think will come of this," Will shook his head.

"Will, we couldn't be bothered to notice that things were going so wrong when he was alive, in time to stop it. So, the least we can do now is acknowledge that we let him down and offer our apologies for not giving him the attention or help he needed." He paused, then said, "Maybe we can even promise to do better for the rest of us. There is so little truth in my family, Will. Maybe if there were more, George wouldn't be dead."

"You won't bring him back," Will said.

"No, but we can make sure his death isn't just some social shame we brush under the rug, even among ourselves. I'm sick of hiding things—everything, it seems, all the time. The cost is too high."

At that moment, two couples pushed past the two men on the sidewalk.

"Excuse me, sir," one of the men said.

"Pardon me," Haydn responded, glancing at the man. His head jerked when he saw who was with the man, arm-in-arm. "Rina!"

The foursome stopped, and Rina looked at Haydn.

Her eyes flashed, but she said formally, "Oh, hello. How are you?"

"I'm...fine. And you?" Haydn's face went hot.

"Fine, thank you," Rina said. An uncomfortable silence descended, and Frederick extended his hand to Haydn.

"Frederick Schulte," he said.

"My husband," Rina added. Haydn shook Frederick's hand, but his eyes stayed on Rina. "And these are our friends, John and Melanie," she motioned to the other couple. "Frederick, this is Haydn Winters, a customer from the dress shop. He brings in items for his mother and sister sometimes."

"I didn't realize you had married," Haydn said, staring at her. "Congratulations."

"Thank you," Frederick said. "We have been celebrating even more good news tonight. I'm going to be a father!"

Frederick beamed. Melanie glanced at Rina with a cautious expression, but Rina did not look at her. Rina kept her eyes on Haydn's face, which had contorted into a struggle between pain, surprise, and an attempt to hide both of those emotions.

"That's wonderful news for you," he said quietly. "Really wonderful."

"Thank you, sir!" Frederick said, and hugged Rina's shoulder. She kept her eyes on Haydn. A beat of silence passed, and Will nudged Haydn.

"Well, it was a pleasure to see you," Haydn said to Rina, "and a pleasure to meet all of you," he nodded at the rest of the party. "Have a pleasant evening."

Haydn pushed through the gate, and Will followed. When they reached the front door, Haydn looked back at the foursome. They had resumed walking down the street, and Haydn watched as they rounded the corner. Just as they disappeared by a building, he saw Rina glance back over her shoulder at him.

CHAPTER 25

AUGUST 30, 1900

"Margaret, how nice to see you," Beatrice said. Margaret could tell she meant it, and somehow that made her feel worse—that and Beatrice's appearance. It wasn't that Bea wasn't keeping herself up. She was doing her hair, dressing stylishly, etc. But she was very thin, and she was pale with dark circles under her eyes. It was clear that she wasn't eating or sleeping.

"I've missed you," Margaret said, hugging Bea's narrow frame.

"I've missed you, too, more than I can say."

Margaret was the one who had come calling, but now she couldn't think what to say. After Peter's report of her at the funeral, Margaret had wanted to check in on Bea, but seeing her, Margaret couldn't bear to ask how she was doing. That was obvious. And asking about Lloyd somehow seemed in bad taste, though Margaret wasn't sure why. So, what was left? The weather? As she struggled to think of something to say, though, Bea rescued her.

"So, tell me about this engagement of yours," Bea said, taking her hand and guiding her to the couch. "It's the talk of the town."

"Can you believe it? Two days and everyone already knows!" Margaret said, smiling. "It's really wonderful, though. Or, at least, I think it is. A part of me wonders what I'm doing!"

"You love him?" Bea asked.

"Oh yes. There's no question of that," Margaret nodded. "Peter is kind and strong and patient. He never asks me to be different than I am, or tells me I won't be able to paint anymore, or that I must fit some sort of mold. I've never had anyone in my life who just loved me as I am, except George."

As soon as George's name tumbled from her mouth, she regretted it. Bea's face scrunched with pain.

"Oh Bea, I—"

"He really did, you know. He loved you with no conditions," Bea said.

"I'm so sorry," Margaret's face crumbled. "I didn't mean to bring up a painful subject!"

"Don't you dare be sorry," Bea said to Margaret. "I'd just die if we could never talk about him again."

"I just…I…" Margaret began to cry.

Bea took her by the shoulders. "Now you listen to me. You have nothing to be sorry about. If we could never say his name again, that would hurt me worse than remembering him does. I loved George more than anyone on this Earth. And I always will. I'll never stop loving him. Do you hear me? Never. And I won't pretend for anyone that he never existed."

"Then why?" Margaret looked confused and looked around furtively. "I mean, why Lloyd?"

"George had demons, Margaret," Bea said. She stood and walked to the front window. With her back to Margaret, she stared outside. "They danced in his head and on his shoulders, and they whispered to him and screamed at him and never gave him a moment's peace. He couldn't outrun them, and he couldn't drown them out, and he was destined to end the way he did."

She turned back around and met Margaret's eye. "There wasn't a thing I could do about it, and I couldn't stand by and watch it. It was too painful. Can you understand that?"

Margaret nodded, though she was not sure she really did understand.

"Some kind of accident, one way or another, was fated," Bea went on. "It couldn't have ended any other way."

"I don't know about that," Margaret looked away.

"Well, I do." Bea stood tall with her hands clasped in front of her.

Margaret began to cry again, and Bea took her again in a hug. The two women embraced for several minutes, until Margaret stopped crying. She sniffled and tried to catch her breath. When she had control of herself, Bea released her.

"I don't know when the last tear will be shed, Margaret," Bea said. "Maybe never. But we'll both stop eventually. If for no other reason, we will stand strong again because we have good men who will hold us up when we need it and let us fall when we need to."

"Lloyd does that for you?" Margaret asked.

"He does," Bea said, a smile easing across her face. "He is strong and steady and so sure that everything will be well that when I feel my foundation starting to give way, just him holding me makes the ground beneath me solid again." She took Margaret's hand. "Does Peter do that for you, Margaret? Does he calm the seas for you when the wind whips them up?"

Margaret thought for a moment.

"I believe that he does," she conceded. She hadn't really thought about Peter's effect on her in those terms, but when Bea put it that way, it felt exactly right.

"Then what is it that makes you question marrying

him?"

"I don't really question it," Margaret said. "I mean, I know it's the right thing. But I guess a part of me is still a little afraid."

"Of what?" Bea persisted.

"I'm afraid that he'll change after we marry," Margaret said. "I'm afraid that despite what he says now, he'll ask me to become something else once I'm his wife. What if once he has me, it's not really me that he wants anymore? What if all this is just about catching the wild bird and then caging it?"

Bea nodded. "I see. Well, I don't know Peter that well, so as much as I'd like to assure you that would never happen, I can't. It seems to me that you'll have to ask the only one who knows. You and Peter need to have a conversation."

"What if he breaks off the engagement?"

"If he breaks off the engagement because you tell him that the Margaret he marries is the one he'll be married to, then it's a gift," Bea patted her hand.

Margaret nodded, but her brow remained furrowed.

"Go talk to Peter," Bea said. "You tell him what you told me. If he is the man you think he is, he won't flinch. And you buck up. That young man fell in love with a spitfire, and I want to see some flames next time I see you."

Margaret laughed, and Bea smiled.

"George always did say you were bossy," Margaret said. And for the first time since George's death, Bea laughed.

* * *

Despite the late night before at the boxing exhibition, Haydn woke early and spent the morning observing the members of his household, trying to figure out who might know what he was sure he knew about George's death, and who might admit it if pushed.

At first, he lingered at the breakfast table, trying to spark conversations about George and gauging the reaction of those around the table. That didn't get him very far. His mother and father refused to say anything, taking great interest in their breakfasts, and Margaret had left quickly after eating, saying she was going to visit a friend. Jefferson seemed nervous and wouldn't come back into the dining room. From that reaction, Haydn assumed even the servants knew the truth, and yet no one would talk.

He would have to talk to people individually.

He decided his father would be a waste of time. They had been alone in the house for weeks, and Haydn had tried numerous times to draw any information he could from Joseph to no avail. Any further attempts would just make him angry.

So, he tried Mildred. He found her sewing in the parlor. He walked into the room, shuffling his feet to announce his presence, but she kept her attention on her sewing. He tried coughing, again with no response from his mother. He then walked in front of her, slumped into a chair and sighed loudly.

Mildred did not look up, but she finally spoke.

"Can I assume from this intrusion that you want something?"

"No, no, I don't want anything," Haydn said, trying to sound casual.

Her fingers worked the needle and thread methodically.

"I mean," Haydn went on, "it's not as if I want you to give me anything or do anything. Not like wanting something in that sense."

She tied off the thread she was working, cut it, then held up a new strand and worked it through the eye of the needle. When it was clear she was not going to take his bait, he continued.

"I can't say I don't want anything, though. If I had my druthers, George would still be alive, and I'd be getting ready to go to Virginia, and everything would be like it was. So, I want that, I suppose."

Mildred began to work the needle and new thread through the fabric. She cast a sideways glance at him, but said nothing.

"It all seems so wrong, don't you think?" he asked. "Like it needn't have happened. Like we could've stopped it."

Mildred dropped her sewing to her lap and looked directly at him. For a moment, she just stared. Haydn felt her assessing him, then she spoke in a tone he couldn't identify. It wasn't anger, but it wasn't sorrow either.

"What are you saying?" she asked. "Exactly, what are you saying?"

The cold edge in her voice unnerved him.

"I just mean…well, that it seems we could have done…something," he stammered.

"If there were anything I could have done, I would have done it," Mildred said, still holding his eye. "I would have thrown myself underneath him to break the fall if I could have. I'd have thrown someone else under him if they'd been within reach. There's nothing I wouldn't have done. But it was out of my hands. It was in someone else's hands, and all I could do was watch—watch my boy, my first-born, die in front of me. Can you fathom that?"

She said the last words slowly and distinctly.

"You saw it? You saw him fall?" Haydn asked.

But rather than answer Haydn's questions, she said, "There was nothing I could do then, and if there were anything I could do now, I would do it. Turn back time. Make a sacrifice to the devil. But there's nothing. I would trade anything and anyone to have George back—anyone," this last word she emphasized, looking at Haydn with hard eyes. "But there's no bargain to be made."

With that, she picked her sewing up and dropped her eyes to it, concentrating on each stitch and dismissing Haydn so completely, he dared not say another word. He felt like he'd been stung in the center of his chest by something small and vicious.

CHAPTER 26

SEPTEMBER 3, 1900

After the exchange with Mildred, Haydn had stood in his bedroom, looking at the window and wondering if he should leave Galveston and simply not come back at all. If Mildred really felt that way—and maybe his father, too—then what was he doing here? He'd given up the only thing that mattered to him to help his family, and no one seemed to appreciate him.

He didn't know why his mother was so hateful at times. His grandmother had told him once that he shouldn't take Mildred's moods personally. She said Mildred didn't know how to be happy, and she lashed out at the people close to her because they were safe targets. They wouldn't, or couldn't, leave her, even if she acted beastly sometimes. Haydn had thought at the time that seemed terribly unfair, and now he thought that maybe he'd had enough.

He crossed his arms and decided he wasn't going to ask any more questions about what had happened to George. His mother's words had been too painful, and he didn't think he could stand any more pain. Mildred's barbs had been almost as painful as seeing Rina—almost.

He thought about Rina and laid down on the bed, hugging a pillow. How could Rina be married to someone else? It felt like just yesterday he'd been holding her in his arms at the beach apartment. He couldn't even think of courting someone else yet, and she was married? Had he meant nothing to her?

He couldn't stand to think about running into Rina again, and if his mother didn't want him here because he was some sort of reminder that the wrong son had died, well, then, maybe he'd just go. Joseph could find someone else to help at the bank. What did he really owe anyone?

Yes. Maybe it was time to just get off of this island of pain. He decided to go tell Joseph right now that he didn't want to stay on at the bank. He wanted to go to school in Virginia like they'd planned before George's accident. He'd figure out a long-term plan once he was in Virginia and away from all this tumult.

He got up from the bed and walked out of his room.

He saw one of Margaret's hairpins on the carpet in the hallway and took it to Margaret's bedroom to return it. When he entered the room, he saw Sallie taking a dress from Margaret's closet.

"Is Margaret going somewhere tonight?" he asked, more to make conversation than out of actual interest.

Sallie jumped, startled, then said, "No sir, she just don't want the dress no more. It's the one from the night she...I mean, the night Mr. George died. She want it burned."

"Burned?" Haydn was taken aback. "Why would she burn her dress?"

"I guess it remind her of what happened. She don't want no reminders of that night. I know I'd burn from my mind what I saw if I could." Her voice became softer when she spoke the last sentence, and Haydn's curiosity prickled. When he tried to talk to her before about George's death, she had run away. But now, she seemed like she *wanted* to tell him something about it. He felt his resolve to ask no more questions quietly melt away.

"What did you see?" he asked, leaning his hip on the vanity just inside the door, trying to appear casual.

"The worst thing I ever seen," Sallie said, tears leaking from her eyes as she stared past Haydn at nothing.

Haydn let her dwell for a moment on whatever scene was clearly replaying itself in her mind. Then after several seconds, he asked quietly, "Did you see George fall?"

Sallie started to say something, then Haydn saw panic creep into her eyes.

"No, no, I didn't see that," she said. She wrapped her arms around herself. "I never said I saw that. I just mean the sight of Mr. George on the stairs. That's all I saw. It was awful. And Mrs. Winters, so upset and screaming. That's what I mean. That's all I saw."

Sallie ran out of the room before Haydn could say anything else. But Haydn knew that wasn't all she had seen. She'd seen *it*. She had seen George fall. She could tell him what he wanted to know. And suddenly, he was overwhelmed again with the need to know. What had happened to George? He had to know. And he wasn't going anywhere until he found out.

* * *

"There's my lovely wife-to-be," Peter smiled as Margaret descended the stairs.

"Happy Labor Day, fiancé," Margaret said.

"I love that Labor Day means a day without labor," Peter said, taking her hand. "They should call it No Labor Day. What would you like to do on this fine No Labor Day? Go for a carriage ride down by the beach?"

"That is tempting. This heat is stifling, and the breeze would certainly be nice."

"Let's go, then."

"Not just yet," Margaret caught Peter's arm. "Let's talk a bit first. Then, if you still want a carriage ride, I'm all yours."

"I hope you're all mine now," he grinned.

"Let's go to the sun porch, Casanova," she said and led him down the hall.

"I've never been in here before," Peter said when they entered the glass-enclosed room. "It's quite nice."

"I'm glad you like it. And I hope you will have many more opportunities to come in here over the next 60 years." She sat on a padded bench and motioned for Peter to sit next to her.

"What do you mean you *hope* I will?"

"I mean that after you hear what I have to say, I hope you will still want to be my husband." She patted the seat next to her again, and Peter sat down. He took her hand.

"There's nothing that could stop me from wanting that," he said.

"I hope that's true. I really do. Because that's what I want, Peter. I want to be with you, and no one else, exactly as you are, forever."

"I've never seen you this serious," Peter said, squeezing her hand.

"I need you to want the same thing."

"I do."

"Do you? Do you really?" Margaret looked hard into

Peter's eyes. "Because I don't think I could be much different than I am, even if I wanted to be, which I don't."

"Why would I want you to be different?"

"Because many people in this city expect the wife of a prominent man to act like a good society wife, like my mother or like yours. So after we're married, they will expect me to host the right kind of parties, with the right kinds of people, and do the right kinds of social activities. And I don't have much interest in all those ridiculous obligations. In case you hadn't noticed, I'm not much for convention," Margaret said, unable to suppress a sly smile.

"I wouldn't say I'm prominent," Peter said, shrugging. "My father is prominent; my mother is prominent. But I've done little to distinguish myself. I don't know how much expectation there would be on me or my wife."

"Don't be modest with me, Peter," Margaret said, dropping the smile and putting her hands on her hips. "I've grown up in the same kind of family you have. I know the rules, and I've never cared much about them. But that's me. I don't care if people don't like it. Are you sure that you could be married to someone who didn't always follow the rules? Could you be happy if I did or said something your mother didn't like or that your friends didn't think I should? Because I probably will,

Peter. I'm not going to suddenly become the proper society matron just because you put a ring on my finger."

"Thank god for that," Peter said. "If you did, I'd be sorely disappointed."

"You would?" Margaret said, wanting to believe him, but still a little doubtful.

"Absolutely. I'm not the least bit interested in marrying my mother or yours. I love my mother. Don't misunderstand. But I'd be bored silly playing all the little games and jumping through all the hoops they do all the time. Why do you think I chose you, dear girl? I need to spend the rest of my life with someone who is going to kick the hoops over with me."

Relief washed over Margaret, and she smiled broadly.

"Then, Mr. Martin, you have chosen well," she said and jumped onto his lap. She kissed him hard, and then softly, on the mouth. "Now, what would you say to knocking over some of those hoops right away?"

"What did you have in mind?" he asked, glancing around.

"I don't want to wait for the big wedding my mother is planning."

"You don't?"

"No. I want to get married now. This weekend. Saturday would be a fine day for a wedding, don't you think?"

She could see that Peter was surprised, but not upset.

And after a beat to absorb the change in plans, he said, "As fine a day as I could imagine."

CHAPTER 27

SEPTEMBER 7, 1900

"I'm going to go for a walk," Haydn announced to Stefan.

"Now? It's only ten-thirty. If your father comes back from his meeting before then, what shall I tell him?"

"Tell him I was hungry and went to lunch early," Haydn said. He realized he sounded short and said, "I won't be gone long, Stefan. I just need to clear my head a bit." Stefan nodded.

Haydn stepped out into the sunlight, took a left and started walking with no particular destination in mind. He just had to get out of the bank for a bit. He had decided that tomorrow would be the day to confront Sallie, and the excitement—or maybe it was anxiety—had left him fidgeting all morning long. He hoped that thinking through his plan for the confrontation might help him calm down. As he walked, he reviewed each step.

When he got up tomorrow, he would tell his father he didn't feel well and wouldn't be coming to the bank. His father wouldn't like it, but there wouldn't be much he could do. With George gone, Haydn was all Joseph had in terms of a successor for the bank, at least for the time being. So if Haydn needed a day off, Joseph would just have to live with that. It's not as if Joseph could afford to fire him.

He tried to rehearse what he would say to Sallie, but he kept changing his mind about the right words. He fingered his earlobe, and his pace slowed. The confrontation was going to be unpleasant, but Haydn kept telling himself how wonderful it would be to have the matter resolved.

Finally, we will all know the truth, he thought. *Everything is going to be better after tomorrow. I can feel it.*

He looked skyward, imagining that Nana was looking down on him, giving him strength. He passed the Levy Building and saw the Weather Chief raising a red flag with a black center. Above the red flag a white pennant flapped in a north wind.

"Is there a storm coming, Mr. Tillery?" Haydn asked.

"It would appear so," Sam Tillery said, pulling a piece of paper out of his pocket. "We received this telegram from the Washington, D.C. Weather Bureau. They say there's a tropical storm south of Louisiana, moving northwest."

"Well, it might be nice to get some rain," Haydn said. "Maybe it will cool things off." The previous night had been unusually hot, more than 90 degrees. Today was also shaping up to be hot as well, despite a north wind.

"Could be," the Weather Chief said. "But I'm not sure I like how the water in the Gulf is rising, considering this north wind. It shouldn't rise like that against an opposing wind."

"Well, I guess you would know," Haydn said. He looked at his pocket watch and realized he had been gone longer than he had intended. "Good luck with your flags," he said and ran back to the bank.

* * *

That evening, Margaret and Peter sat on the front porch at Painter House.

"My word, the heat!" Margaret said, fanning herself.

"My delicate flower," Peter teased.

"You're going to see how delicate I am if you keep that up," Margaret said, giving him a mock warning look and hitting him with her fan. She wondered how men got by in the summer without fans. "I would have thought that the sun setting would help the heat, but it just doesn't seem to be cooling off."

"The breeze helps," Peter said. "And look at that sky. That's got to be one of the most beautiful sunsets I've ever seen. It's like the whole sky has been painted crimson!"

"It's a sign," Margaret said.

"Of what?"

"Of the bright future we're going to have after tomorrow," Margaret said, getting up from her seat and taking his hand. "Is everything ready?" she asked with her voice lowered.

"I have a bag packed and hidden under my bed," Peter said, lowering his voice to match hers and leaning his head near Margaret's. "Tomorrow, I'll go to work in the morning, like always, but at lunch, I'll tell my father I'm not feeling well and excuse myself for the rest of the day. I'll go straight to the train station and buy us tickets to Houston. Can you be there by 12:30?"

"With bells on," Margaret grinned. Her stomach was full of butterflies, and she was sure she wouldn't sleep a wink tonight. Tomorrow couldn't get here soon enough.

"That's my girl!" Peter said and kissed her forehead. "We can be in Houston and married before anyone is even done with work for the day. No fuss and no parents. We can send a telegram from Houston that we've eloped, and on Sunday, we can come back and figure out what to do for a real honeymoon. Two days in a swamp is not what I call a honeymoon for any wife of mine."

"Houston may be a swamp, but it'll be our wedding swamp, so we'll have to speak more kindly of it in the future," Margaret said.

"Whatever you say, dear."

"Oh, I like how this marriage is starting," Margaret smiled. Peter took her fan and hit her hair with it, and Margaret laughed. His face turned serious, and he took both of her hands.

"You are sure this is how you want to do this?" he asked.

"Absolutely," she said and squeezed his hands. And she meant it.

CHAPTER 28

SEPTEMBER 8, 1900

"Be careful, love," Frederick said, holding Rina's hand and guiding her over the dunes.

"You're sweet," Rina said. "I don't think the baby is in any danger from me walking along the beach, but I love that you're concerned." She did love that Frederick was attentive. She'd been working hard since they married to use the word love in any context she could. She didn't yet feel that she was in love with Frederick, but she hoped that if she focused enough on the things she loved, or even liked, the feeling would grow.

"The neighbors weren't exaggerating, were they?" he said looking at the surf. "Look at the swells!"

"They are impressive," Rina agreed.

"You would do better to be apprehensive instead of impressed," a man said behind them. They turned to see S. O. Young, the secretary of the Galveston Cotton Exchange.

"Good morning, Mr. Young," Frederick said. "The newspaper said we'd have rain for the next couple of days then it would clear. Why should we be apprehensive?"

"Because you can expect a damn sight more than just rain," Young said. "It's not just a little storm coming. It's a cyclone."

"A cyclone?" Rina said and grabbed Frederick's arm.

"Oh, I don't think it will be that serious," Frederick said to Rina, patting her arm. "Look at the children playing in the swells. They're having a wonderful time!"

"Children are hardly the ones who would know," Young said.

"Well, how do you know it's a cyclone?" Frederick said, a note of aggravation creeping into his voice.

"Because just a little while ago, I watched the tide completely wash over that track," he said, pointing to a street railway track that ran along the beach. "That's not normal. I'm telling you, it's a cyclone."

Rina felt fear start to creep into her stomach.

"You can stay and watch things worsen if you like, but I'm going to go cable my wife," Young said. "She's on her way here this morning by train, and I'm going to tell her to get off in San Antonio instead and wait." He pointed a finger at Frederick and said, "If you were smart, you'd get your wife off this beach and get her to high ground while you can."

Young turned and walked quickly away. "Frederick, is there something we should do to prepare?" Rina asked. "Should we leave the Island? I've never seen a cyclone, but I know they're dangerous."

"Mr. Young is making mountains out of molehills," he told her, patting her arm again. "He doesn't work for the Weather Bureau. What does he know? I'm sure this is nothing more than an overflow."

Rina bit her lip and looked at the swells.

"Look, I don't want you to worry," Frederick said. "Let's go home, secure the house, and then I'll take you to the store with me. You can spend the day there. Mr. Klaussen won't mind, and it's farther from the beach, so it will be safer if there's flooding."

Rina nodded, and they started walking back to their house. A block from the beach, she saw a two-wheeled bathhouse lying on its side. She knew that meant the tide swells had lifted it and deposited it there before pulling back into the sea, and she frowned.

Her fear increased when she saw Samuel Tillery drive by in a cart, looking anxiously from his watch to the swells coming ashore.

* * *

A few hours later, Rina watched as Frederick picked up a box from the floor of the store and climbed a ladder. He placed the box onto a shelf several feet up off the floor. It was mid-morning, and there was a steady rain outside the store windows that seemed to have no interest in slacking.

She had seen this ritual before. When flooding was expected, they moved the merchandise to shelves at least three feet off the floor to keep it from being ruined by the flood waters. Some of the low-lying areas of the island were already flooded, so Mr. Klaussen said he wanted to take no chances.

A woman stepped inside, thoroughly soaked, and reported that the waves at the beach were quite impressive and a crowd had gathered.

"The waves are crashing against the streetcar trestles and shooting into the air," she'd enthused. "It's quite grand!"

"That's not the word I would use," Mr. Klaussen said, as he handed Frederick another box.

Rina didn't think it was the word she would use, either. She knew that overflows were common, but something felt different this time, and she didn't like the feeling.

* * *

At 11:00 a.m., Peter called Margaret at home.

"How is your packing progressing, my girl?"

"It's a little slow. I'm trying to do it discreetly, and that's not easy around here. Between Mother and the servants, there are too many eyes. And wouldn't you know Haydn stayed home from the bank today? But I'm working on it and on my letter to Mother as well. I'm glad I won't be here when she reads it."

"Me, too!" Peter laughed.

"Incidentally, have you looked outside in the last little while? It's really coming down," Margaret said, looking out the window.

"Yes, I know! I've heard that people are gathering at the Midway to watch the sea. One of my father's employees said the waves are smashing the bathhouses, and I've heard some railway trestles have been unearthed, though I don't know that I believe that."

"Railway trestles? You don't think we'll have any trouble getting to Houston, do you?" Margaret twisted the phone cord in her hand.

"No, no," Peter said. "I think people are just getting excited and exaggerating things. There is some flooding, but I can't imagine that rail service will be disrupted. I should go now, but I'll call you again when I get home."

Margaret no sooner hung up the phone when it rang again.

"What's going on over there?" Joseph demanded.

"Sir?" Margaret asked confused.

"I've been trying to call for 15 minutes. Who has been on the phone?"

"What were you calling about?" Margaret said, evading his question.

"It's flooding," Joseph said. "Gulf water has reached all the way to Avenue K, and some of my customers have told us water is waist-deep in some parts of the city. So, I'm closing the bank. Without Haydn here it's hard to get anything done anyway, so I'm coming home. Tell Jefferson to have lunch prepared when I get there."

"Yes, sir," Margaret said, pursing her lips and replacing the receiver.

CHAPTER 29

SEPTEMBER 8, 1900

Haydn entered the kitchen as silently as possible. He had been unable to sleep last night, fretting about the confrontation with Sallie, so he had gone to the beach this morning to try to walk off some of his restlessness. Looking at the signs of the coming storm had only increased his anxiety, though, and he was ready to get the encounter over.

Sallie stood at the sink, her back to the room, filling the pot for coffee. He surmised that his father must be coming home, because Mildred rarely drank coffee at lunch. He would have to hurry.

"Hello, Sallie," he said.

The young girl jumped and dropped the lid of the

coffee pot into the sink with a clatter. Snatching it back up, she looked over her shoulder at Haydn.

"You startled me, sir. Can I get you something?"

"No, thank you" he said, trying to sound casual. He crossed the kitchen and reached a hand out. "Here, let me help you with that."

"Oh, no, sir," she said, putting the lid on the pot. "I can do it. I do this by myself every day, and besides, if Missus Mildred saw you helping she'd be very upset."

"Well, we wouldn't want her to be upset. There's been enough of that the last few months, hasn't there?"

Sallie glanced at him then returned her gaze to the coffee pot. "Yes, sir. I suppose there has."

"It's very difficult to lose a child. Worse than losing a brother, I should think."

"I guess I wouldn't know," Sallie said, loading scoops of coffee into the machine.

"There isn't much worse than losing George," he said. "The only thing that could make it worse is if the circumstance under which he died was something different from what everyone says it was—something worse."

Sallie stared at the coffee pot. "I don't think I understand you, sir."

"I think you do, Sallie."

They stood in silence for a beat, then Haydn continued.

"I think you know what happened the night George died, Sallie, and I think it wasn't a simple accident like Father and I were told. Or maybe it's just me that's been told that. I don't know who knows what anymore. Except that I think you know it wasn't just a fall down the stairs, don't you? In fact, I think you saw the fall, didn't you, Sallie?"

Tears formed in the girl's eyes. She dropped her head and tried to protest. "No, that's not right. I didn't see nuthin', sir."

Haydn touched her shoulder. She flinched, but Haydn didn't let go.

"It's okay, Sallie," he said with a soft voice. "I won't tell Mrs. Winters that you told me. I won't tell her that you were watching George the night he died or that you know the real story. I won't tell anyone anything. Just tell me exactly what you saw, and it'll stay between you and me."

Sallie stood perfectly still, tears now running down her face, but she didn't say a word.

Haydn knew time was ticking by. His father was coming home, and he would expect to eat as soon as he came through the door, which meant Jefferson would be coming into the kitchen any minute to prepare lunch.

"You were upstairs the night George died, weren't you, Sallie?" he pressed. Sallie didn't correct him. "You saw everything, didn't you?"

After what seemed like an eternity to Haydn, Sallie dropped her head and nodded, almost imperceptibly. Haydn felt his heart begin to beat faster. He struggled to keep his voice level.

"What did you see, Sallie? What happened?"

"Oh, Mr. Haydn. It was the most awful thing I ever saw," she buried her face in her hands.

She proceeded to tell Haydn what she saw in a rushed voice.

She had been upstairs putting away laundry in a linen closet when she heard Margaret yelling.

"I won't do it, Mother! I won't!" Margaret slammed her hand on the banister at the top of the stairs and glared down at Mildred who was standing downstairs in the foyer.

"You most certainly will," Mildred said in a hard, modulated voice.

"I'm not a slave! You can't sell me to the highest bidder."

"And you're not Bettie Brown. You're not going to embarrass this family by gallivanting around this town and through life as some scandalous old maid!"

"That's exactly what I'm going to do!" Margaret's eyes flashed.

"Over my dead body!" Mildred stamped her foot.

"Don't I wish," Margaret screamed.

George entered the foyer from the study, a glass of whiskey in one hand, gesturing palm up with the other. "Ladies, please," he said. "You're going to bring down the whole house."

"That's just fine!" Margaret shouted. "Without a mansion on Broadway, maybe I'd be a less valuable cow on the market."

"Reason with her, George," Mildred pleaded.

George obliged and mounted the stairs unsteadily. "Now, Margie, you know you'd be a perfectly valuable cow even without Painter House as part of the dowry."

"Shut up, George! There's not going to be a dowry, with or without Painter House. I'm not getting married—ever!"

"I thought you liked Peter," he said, making his way up the stairs.

"That's neither here nor there," she glared at him. "I'm not going to be a servant to any man, like or not, love or not. And I'm not going to be some pawn in Mother's game of social chess. It's not going to happen!"

"It's love, then?" George raised his eyebrows. He put his foot on the top step and reached out for Margaret's shoulder, dropping his voice so that only Margaret could hear him. "Margie, listen to me. If you love this boy, don't let Mother be a consideration. Don't sacrifice your own happiness to spite her. Marry this boy if that's what you want."

"Everyone just leave me alone!" she screamed and shoved George in the chest. She turned to run, but stopped at the sound of a muted grunt and a thud. She spun around to see George lying on the landing. In what seemed like slow motion, his glass thumped down the stairs then shattered on the marble below.

Sallie saw Margaret stand in place for a moment, staring at the scene below her, then she screamed the most terrifying scream Sallie had ever heard. No one moved for several seconds, then Mildred ran to George.

"George! George!" she touched his face. "Oh my God, oh my God! Margaret, what did you do?"

Margaret turned and ran to her room, slamming the door behind her. She never saw Sallie standing to her right, cowering in the linen closet doorway, her hand over her mouth.

CHAPTER 30

SEPTEMBER 8, 1900

Haydn stood motionless, staring at Sallie. The girl was weeping openly now, her face in her hands.

"He...he didn't...you mean that Margaret...," he struggled to find the words, to wrap his mind around what Sallie had just told him. George had not committed suicide. George had been murdered, pushed down the stairs by his own sister.

No, not murdered, he corrected himself silently. That suggested intent. Nothing in Sallie's account indicated intent. *It had been an accident—a horrible, horrible accident. My God, what Margaret must have been feeling all this time,* he thought, staggering backward and grabbing the counter.

The sound of footsteps approaching the kitchen

caused Sallie to rush to the sink and turn on the water. She splashed her face and wiped it with a dishtowel. Haydn grasped the counter and looked at the floor.

Jefferson entered the kitchen.

"Oh, hello, sir," the older man said to Haydn. "I was about to put together some lunch for your father. Would you like something?"

Haydn looked up. He was slow to respond, but finally said, "No, thank you, Jefferson. I need to go. Thank you," he said again and rushed out of the room before Jefferson could respond.

* * *

Margaret opened a drawer, pawed through its contents, shut it, then opened it again and stared at the mussed clothes. Outside her window, rain was gushing from the skies as if a giant pail had been dumped from the heavens, and the electricity was out.

She heard a knock downstairs at the front door, then her father's voice saying, "Peter! What a surprise. Did your father close for the day as well?"

"Well, sir, the island is flooded all the way to 12th Street, and the streetcars have ceased running, so it seemed like time to call it a day," Peter said. "With things starting to get a bit out of hand with this storm, I wanted to check in on Margaret."

"She's in her room, I believe," Joseph gestured up the stairs. "You can go up if you like. Elinor is upstairs lighting candles, so Margaret is not alone."

She heard him pound up the stairs then knock on her door. She opened the door and craned her head around him. "Did anyone else come up with you?" she whispered.

"Not that I'm aware of," he whispered back.

"Good!" she said, and let him into the room. She couldn't shut the door all the way with Peter in the room, but she angled it as far as she could to obscure the view into her room. She shoved a suitcase under her bed.

"Elinor has been trying to get in here for 20 minutes, and I keep putting her off," Margaret said. "I needed to finish packing."

"I don't think you need to worry about that," Peter said, sitting on the edge of the bed. "I don't see any way that we can get out to Houston."

"Oh no!" she said. "Are you sure?"

"The weather has gotten too bad, I'm afraid. From what I'm hearing, the Midway has been destroyed, and the bathhouses are about to be swallowed by the Gulf. I tried to go take a look myself, but it wasn't safe, so I had to give up. I did see that people who live near the beach, though, are cutting holes in the floors of their houses to try and stabilize them against the rising water."

Margaret sat back on the windowsill. This couldn't

be happening.

"On my way here, I heard some men say that the north wind was causing flooding from the other side of the island as well and jostling the train cars," Peter continued. "That means the island is flooding in from both sides, love. I don't think the railway trestles are safe anymore."

"We've flooded before, lots of times," Margaret said. "Do you really think this is different?"

"I do. I don't know how bad it's going to get, but I know this isn't normal. And I know it wouldn't be safe to try and leave tonight. Let's just let this thing wash out, and maybe tomorrow we can try again."

Margaret lowered her head and nodded. Peter kissed her on the head.

"I'll stay with you here," he said. "There's no reason to trudge back through the water to get to my house. Besides, wherever you are is where my home is now, wedding band or not." At this she raised her face and smiled at him.

"Let's go get some coffee downstairs," she said.

When they walked into the kitchen, they found a stranger at the table usually occupied by Jefferson or a member of his family. Jefferson was serving him coffee.

"We have a guest?" Margaret asked.

"This is Thomas Porter," Jefferson explained, gesturing at the bedraggled man. "He live near the beach, and he had to leave. Some man came riding down the street in a cart telling everyone to 'vacuate. But he didn't have nowhere to go. The rest of his family all live near where he do, and everything is under water. He know me and Elinor live here, so he just came here. I hope it's okay if he stays for a little while—just till the water back off. He'll stay right in here and be quiet."

Margaret wondered if Mildred knew about this. When she didn't say anything right away, Jefferson added, "He tried at the Martin house, because he know some folks on they staff."

"But they told me no," the man spoke up. "They said they wasn't in the business of taking in strays."

Peter's face turned red. Margaret straightened her back and said to Jefferson, "Well, of course, he can stay. And from what Peter has told me, there may be many more people in trouble before this is over, and we're on high ground. So anyone else who comes looking for shelter will also be welcome."

"They most certainly will not!" Mildred stood in the doorway to the kitchen.

Margaret looked back to Jefferson. "Make sure we have enough coffee and blankets. People are going to be soaked to the skin."

"Margaret, do we look like a hotel?" Mildred demanded, her hands on her hips.

Haydn entered the kitchen. "Oh!" he said, clearly

surprised at the crowd in the room. "Margaret, I was going to talk to you about something, but it looks like maybe now isn't a good time."

"Mother, Peter says the water is covering the island from both directions, and the storm is getting worse," Margaret said, ignoring Haydn. "People are starting to lose their homes, and they need some place to wait out the rain. I've told Jefferson not to turn anyone away, and—"

"I don't care how hard it's raining, we—" Mildred interrupted.

"Mother! This isn't up for discussion," Margaret shot back. "The Martins are turning people away, and there are only so many places on this island that people can go. I won't allow even one more death on this island if I can do anything to help it!"

At that, Mildred's lips snapped shut. Haydn looked at the two women, squaring off at one another, then at the stranger huddled at the kitchen table. He stepped next to his sister.

"Margaret is right," he said. "This storm is clearly swirling out of control, and we have to do what we can to help. Forget about what people might think, and let's just do what's right from here on out."

Mildred looked at Haydn. They held eyes as understanding passed between them.

"Very well, then," she said. "Someone find Sallie and

tell her to bring linens downstairs. If we're to have water-logged guests, I'd prefer to cover the furniture."

CHAPTER 31

SEPTEMBER 8, 1900

The next several hours passed in a blur of activity and increasing anxiety. When Haydn had heard Margaret stand up to Mildred in the kitchen, he'd felt his resolve to confront her about George evaporate.

Until then, he had thought only of George—finding out what had really happened to his brother and forcing his family to face it. He thought that might somehow absolve them all of not being there for George when he needed them. But with abrupt clarity, he had realized there was no need for him to force anything.

Haydn knew the truth now, and he knew it wasn't about his own self-absorption. Margaret was, in fact, dealing with the truth of George's death. And she would for the rest of her life.

And Mildred? Well, she was doing the best she could. Maybe Joseph was, too.

They all knew what had really happened, and discussing it wasn't going to change anything. The truth was that talking about it would likely just amount to pouring salt into open wounds. He could practically hear George saying, "Let sleeping dogs lie, ol' boy."

So, he threw himself into the situation at hand. As Painter House began to fill with refugees, each new arrival told him a story more harrowing than the last.

"It was just awful," said one man, soaked to the skin and sporting scratches. "I was sloshing through the water, holding on to my daughter with a grip that I'm sure has left bruises." He lifted the arm of a girl standing next to him, about 8 or 9 years old by Haydn's estimate.

"I turned my head to the side, to avoid the rain stinging my face. It's so driven by the wind it feels like needles. And suddenly I saw something fall from a window. I realized just as it hit the water that it was a baby! I looked around to see if someone would follow after the child, but I couldn't see anyone going after her. Or maybe it was a him. I have no way of knowing." Tears were forming in the man's eyes.

"I tried to go after the baby myself, but there was no way. I could not get to her, and even if I could, I couldn't have found her in the water and held on to my daughter.

It was impossible. You see that, don't you? You can see that there was nothing I could do?" The man's eyes, with tears streaming from them now, implored Haydn for absolution.

"Anyone could see that," Haydn said, putting a hand on the man's shoulder. The man held his daughter to his chest and cried openly.

Another man said he had gone to the weather office to try and ask what was happening, but he couldn't get an answer. "The phone was ringing incessantly," he said. "People were calling from all over the island reporting about the conditions, and it sounded positively biblical! They were talking about massive waves pummeling the beach and marching inland, pounding on the front doors of houses. They said bathhouses had been smashed into splinters that were now pushing through the streets. And strangest of all," he said, wide eyes playing to his audience, "some callers reported an inundation of tiny frogs."

"Oh," one woman said and made a disgusted face. Her husband spoke up.

"I work down on Mechanic Street, and I went to Ritter's Café for lunch," he said. "I was talking with a bunch of other businessmen about the cotton exchange and the wharves, just like any other day. And I'll admit, I noticed the waiters looked a little nervous as they took orders and delivered food, but honestly, I was just trying to ignore what was happening outside. We all just pretended we didn't hear the howling wind and we weren't all wet to the gills. I guess the wind took exception, because next thing we knew, it ripped the roof off the building."

"You're joking," Haydn said in disbelief.

"I wish I were, sir," the man said, shaking his head. "We didn't even know it at first. Ritter's is on the first floor of the building, so we could hear that something had happened, but we couldn't see the destruction. But as the wind tore through the print shop above the café, it caused the walls to bow, and the floor gave way. The ceiling, chairs, desks and, worst of all, the heavy presses came smashing down on us. It was horrible!" The man's eyes seemed to glaze over as he recalled the scene.

"People came running to help, and someone dispatched a waiter to find a doctor, but I don't know if he found one. I wanted to stay and help, but I knew I had to find my family. For the first time all day, I really understood how bad this thing is. As I left, a little after two o'clock, I saw the rain gauge blow away off the Levy building. And when I got into the street on Mechanic, the wooden pavers that normally line the streets of the business area were floating like a cotillion of buoys."

"It's like Armageddon," Haydn said.

"I would agree," the man said. "I got home and saw that my house was several feet under water, so I told my wife I wanted to get word out to my brother in Dallas about what's happening. I thought I might need his help when this is over. She said she didn't want us to get separated, so we went together to the Western Union office. They told me they'd been down for two hours, so I tried the Postal Telegraph office. They told me the same thing. Telegraph lines all across the city are down. We tried to make our way back to our house, but we couldn't get back to it. That's how we ended up here."

"Use our phone," Haydn said and pointed to their telephone. "You can call the Western Union office in Houston and get a message out from there."

"Really, sir?" the man asked, looking hopeful.

"Of course," Haydn said.

"That's just grand. Thank you!"

The man jumped up and ran to the phone. He dialed the long-distance number to Houston, but when he was finally connected with the Western Union office there, the operator told him, "I'm sorry, sir. There are four thousand calls ahead of yours. You'll have to try again later."

He hung up and relayed the message to the other people in the room.

"Four thousand calls?" Haydn said. "That can't be right. Let me try."

But when he picked up the phone to call back, the line was dead. He looked out the window and saw that the telephone lines outside had snapped. The island was now cut off from the outside world.

CHAPTER 32

SEPTEMBER 8, 1900

Rina perched on a stool behind the counter at Klaussen's, watching the scene outside the window with increasing concern. Barton Mills entered the shop about 3:00 p.m., looked around at the barren floor and the merchandise hefted a few feet up and muttered to himself, "Not sure that's going to do it."

"Mr. Mills, I'm so glad to see you're alright," Rina said. "I was getting worried."

"I won't mince words," Barton said. "It was mighty rough getting back here. Do you have any idea what's going on out there?" he motioned with his thumb in the direction of the door.

"The collapse at Ritter's? Isn't it just awful?" Rina

said.

"It's more than that," Barton shook his head. "The lighthouse is completely cut off, and water is waist-high at 28th and Broadway."

"That far in? What about the beach?"

"It's part of the ocean at this point," Barton said. "The whole beach front is being abandoned. Some houses are flooding, and others are being broken up like stick forts. People are trying to find higher ground and stronger houses. I passed Samuel Tillery on my way back here, and he was going home to check on his wife and children. As soon as I hand this money from my deliveries to Mr. Klaussen, I'm going to do the same thing."

Frederick and Mr. Klaussen came from the storeroom in time to hear the last of Mills' statement.

"Of course," Mr. Klaussen said, as Mills handed him a handful of cash. "You go on home. I could've waited until tomorrow to get this delivery money from you."

"I wouldn't have been comfortable carrying it around, Mr. Klaussen."

"I understand," he said and pocketed the money. "Well, you go on home."

Mills thanked his boss and headed back out into the driving rain.

"Frederick," Rina said. "What about Papa and Oma? What if they're trapped? Or what if their house is one of the ones that's been knocked down?"

"They live on the second floor, so I'm sure they'll be safe," Frederick said. "Let's just stay where we are and help Mr. Klaussen keep his merchandise dry. As soon as the water recedes, we'll go straight to your father's house."

Rina nodded, but did not feel consoled.

* * *

Melanie looked with concern out the window of her house. Gusts of wind were coming faster, and each seemed to hit harder than the one before.

She wondered if the glass would hold and took a step back from the window. As she did, a sledgehammer of wind bashed into the side of the house, knocking plaster from the wall. Melanie shrieked, and when that gust was quickly followed by another, and plaster fell from the ceiling into her hair, she'd had enough.

"John, I don't want to stay here," she said. The tone of her voice made it clear to John that what she meant was that was she was not going to stay, and he didn't try to argue.

"Where should we go?" he asked.

"Let's go to Daddy's store," she said. "That's sturdy enough for any storm."

The couple stepped out onto the porch and hesitated

momentarily. They had been listening to the wind for sometime, but feeling the force of it was daunting. Melanie felt as if she might be pushed from her feet, and she grabbed John's arm. She felt his body tense with the effort to push back against the wind.

"Let's go," he said, setting his jaw, as if it might fortify him against the wind. He took Melanie by the arm and ushered her down from the porch and into several feet of water covering their small front yard.

They moved into the street and pulled their legs through the river that flowed through their neighborhood. Several other people were doing the same, and some used makeshift walking sticks to push through the current. Melanie wished she had such a stick, but realized that if she did, she wouldn't have a free hand to maneuver it. Her skirts had become heavy with the water, pulling her down toward the sucking earth, and it took both hands and all the strength in her arms to hold them up to keep from tripping on them. Her legs burned with the strain of pushing through the water, and her face stung from the rain, driving down hard from the darkening sky.

She fell twice—once when a surge in the current upset her balance, and once when something large and unidentified below the water pushed her from behind. John never released his grip on her arm and managed to pull her up both times before her head went under the water but not before the top half of her dress became equally sodden and heavy. Each time she stood up, she felt more of her strength sap away.

When they reached Broadway, the couple joined a grim parade of evacuees, heading toward the safety of higher ground. It had taken them nearly an hour to go only a few blocks, and Klaussen's Dry Goods was still several blocks away. They were both exhausted. A large piece of timber slammed into John's leg from within the swirling brown water, leaving his pants torn, and he came to a conclusion.

"We'll never make it to your father's store," he shouted over the scream of the wind.

"What do we do?" Melanie asked, her fear heightened by the fabric of her dress starting to tatter and slap forcefully against her skin.

"There," he said, pointing to a large house, its porch untouched yet by the flood waters. "Go there."

* * *

By 4:00 p.m., the Winters home hosted strangers from all over the island. Haydn knew that some of the evacuees were people who shouldn't have been strangers—people who some member of the family passed on the street or came in contact with every day in some capacity. But others were truly that—visitors to the city or workers who had sailed in on one of the ships now bobbing in the wharf. These travelers knew neither their hosts nor what to expect from the storm now battering the city.

No one called the storm what it was. No one said the word "hurricane." If they said it, it would be true. But no one was calling it an overflow either. They simply called it a storm, though there was nothing simple about this storm, which only increased in ferocity with each passing hour. And by now, it was indeed ferocious.

Haydn stayed near the front door so he could hear if anyone rapped on it looking for shelter from the punishing rain or flooding waters, which had now submerged every inch of the island's surface. He had to stay close by to hear, because the wind was now so loud, it sounded like a freight train was passing over the house at full speed.

Twice he thought he heard knocking and wrestled the door open to find no one there. The second of these times, he noticed Buddy cowering behind a stone planter near the door. The dog looked at Haydn with fearful brown eyes, and Haydn patted his thighs and tried to speak in a soothing voice, even though he had to shout above the wind.

"Come here, boy. Good dog." The dog inched forward, his tail between his legs.

Haydn positioned himself back in the chair by the

closed front door, this time with Buddy by his side.

Again he heard knocking and leaped to the door. When he opened it, he recognized the face looking back at him, despite strands of drenched blonde hair pasted to her cheeks and clothing tattered by the ripping wind.

"Melanie! Come in!"

CHAPTER 33

SEPTEMBER 8, 1900

As the storm raged, evacuees took refuge inside Klaussen's, and Rina was starting to feel claustrophobic as a result of all the bodies, heat, humidity, and fear. With each passing minute, things seemed to get worse, and every ravaged person that made it into the store seemed in worse shape than the last.

The door opened and slammed backward against the wall with the force of a gust. When she looked to see who was coming in, she saw a man teetering in the doorway, his face streaming with blood. A woman helped him into the entry and pulled the door shut behind her.

Rina closed her eyes and took a deep breath to try to calm herself, but she barely expelled the breath when she heard Mr. Klaussen shout, "Rina, please bring me some cloth to press to this wound."

She opened her eyes and saw that Mr. Klaussen was kneeling on the floor cradling the man's head in his lap. The man's head was bleeding profusely from a gash near his temple, and he was unconscious. The man's wife knelt beside him, praying and crying.

Rina snatched a shirt from the shelf behind her and rushed to Mr. Klaussen's side.

"What happened?" she asked the man's wife.

"A tile of slate hit him," the woman said.

"Slate?" Rina asked, confused.

"The wind is ripping them from rooftops and flinging them through the air so hard and so fast, there's no way to duck," the woman explained. "It's as if the gods are shooting axe blades at us with slingshots. And if it's not tiles, it's wooden shutters from windows. Andrew was leading me through the water," she turned her eyes to the unconscious man. "He looked back to see how I was doing, and he was struck full force by one of the tiles.

"The bleeding was immediate, and I could see that he was dazed, but we managed to stagger to your store. He never let go of my hand until he pushed open the door to the store," she said. She looked at her empty hand, then reached down and took her husband's in hers.

"I don't know how he made it," the woman said, looking at her husband, tears mixing with the rainwater that left her face red with pain. "We saw a lot of people with less serious injuries than Andrew's fall under the water. They would get swallowed under, and you'd never see them come back up. I've never been so scared in my life. Until this moment," she said looking at her husband's grey face.

Mr. Klaussen pressed the cloth to the man's head. It filled quickly with blood and Rina brought him a second shirt. This one stained more slowly.

"We've seen people fleeing into any building they could find with an open door. Where are they all coming from?" Rina asked.

Andrew's wife seemed to calm a bit when she saw that the bleeding from her husband's head was subsiding.

"Everywhere, I think, but mostly from any place along the shore," she said. "There are hundreds of people in the Tremont Hotel. We thought we'd try to stick it out and go just a little further, to the Strand. We thought maybe the buildings wouldn't be as crowded. We saw the water sweeping back toward the Gulf, and we thought that meant the water was receding. But it wasn't. The bay water was flooding in and pushing the Gulf water back toward the sea. It's not going down; it's just swirling now, pulling people under. Everything is flooded. And that's not the worst of it."

"What could be worse?" Rina asked, thinking of her father and Oma. She also found herself thinking about

Haydn. Had he made it out of the bank safely? Was he one of the people huddled at the Tremont?

"There's a wall of debris pushing through the streets," the woman answered. "If the storm doesn't tear down your house, the wall will simply smash it underfoot and absorb it. It's a monster, eating everything in its path and just getting stronger. It comes at you with boards, nails, and pipes sticking out of it to tear into anyone and anything it can grab. Andrew and I got ahead of it, but I saw people crushed by it. What I've seen today will never leave me. Never."

Mr. Klaussen continued to hold a cloth to Andrew's head, but Rina stepped away. Frederick had been standing a few feet away. She gripped his arm.

"Frederick, we have to go get Papa and Oma."

"Rina, my love, did you not hear what this lady said? We'll be killed if we go out there."

"Frederick, I cannot live with myself if I sit here safely while Papa and Oma are killed in a storm without us even trying to help them. You can stay here if you like, but I'm going to get my father."

"No," Frederick said, squeezing her hand. "I'll go. You stay here and keep the baby safe."

"I can't," Rina shook her head. "I can't just sit here. I'm going, too."

They heard someone shout, "Here it comes!" A woman was pointing toward the door. Water was beginning to flow under it and into the store. People began to run backward, but Rina rushed forward. She looked out the window. The street had become a sea, or more aptly, part of the Gulf.

"All of the women and children up on the counters," Mr. Klaussen shouted.

Rina pulled the door open, allowing a short rush of water into the store, to the panic of the other people in the store, but with Frederick behind her, she stepped into the swirling water.

CHAPTER 34

SEPTEMBER 8, 1900

Rina and Frederick managed to make it a few blocks before she realized the futility of their mission. They were already bruised and exhausted, and with the landscape scrubbed of many of its usual landmarks, Rina kept losing her bearings on where they should even be going. She stopped where they were and put her hands on her knees, which were under water.

Her hair was plastered around her face, and her mouth hung open as she tried to get enough breath. Their faces had been pelted with shells picked up from the streets and hurled at them by the wind, and she could feel that her face was scratched and bleeding. A long splinter of wood pierced Frederick's arm shortly after they left store, and he was in pain. But Rina knew he didn't want to be the one to call off the rescue mission for her family.

"What do you think?" he called to her over the roar of the wind.

She dropped her chin to her chest, and the rain pounded the back of her head. After a few seconds, she stood up, tears mixing with the rain on her face.

"I can't go any farther," she said. "I just can't."

Frederick put his good arm around her and held her for a moment, then looked around. After a couple of seconds, he pointed to a house about a block away. "Let's go there," he said resolutely. It seemed miles away to Rina.

"Why so far? Why not one of these?" she gestured to two houses closer than the one Frederick indicated.

"The one I'm pointing to is Barton Mills' house," he explained. "I'm not sure anyone else would even open their door at this point, but he'll let us in if he's there."

They set off toward the house.

After what seemed like an eternity, they made it to the porch of Barton's house. They knocked on the front door, and after several seconds, Barton answered.

"Frederick!" he said, surprised. "And Rina? Good lord, child, what are you doing outside? Why aren't you at the store? Frederick, how could you bring her out in this?"

He ushered them inside. When they stepped through

the door, they found the living room full of people. No one said anything when they stumbled inside, but everyone looked at her and Frederick.

"It's not his fault, Mr. Mills," Rina said wearily. "Frederick wanted to stay at the store, but I was afraid for my father and grandmother. I insisted we go to them. It was foolish, and now I'm afraid I've put both of us in jeopardy…and the baby. We didn't know what to do until we saw your house. May we stay here to wait out the storm?"

"Of course, child," Barton said, putting his arm around Rina's shoulder. "But let's have you go upstairs. It's less crowded. My family is up there. You can wait with them for the rain to pass."

"I don't want to leave Frederick," Rina said, holding on to Frederick's arm.

"Both of you go, then," Barton said, gesturing toward the stairs.

"Barton, I don't mean to be forward," Frederick said, "but it's really gotten bad outside. It's only a matter of time until the water floods in. I'm actually surprised it hasn't already. I think you would do well to move everyone upstairs."

Barton looked outside and saw the flood waters inching up the stairs to his porch. "You may be right," he said.

"Well, why don't we move all of your furniture to the

second floor, as well?" Rina said. "I know that will make it crowded, but it would be a shame for any of your valuables to be damaged." Rina didn't know how valuable Barton's possessions were, but from what she and Frederick had just experienced outside, she was sure everyone would be here for a while, and moving the furniture upstairs not only would keep it out of the flood waters, but the activity also would keep everyone's minds off of what was happening outside.

"I suppose it can't hurt," Barton said. He directed the people in the living room into action. Several men rolled up rugs and carried them up the stairs, while women and children picked up whatever items they could and did the same. Everyone moved as many items as they could upstairs, then they sat wherever they could find a place.

Rina found a window with a window seat and sat down. Frederick came and sat by her, and they looked out into the street. A corpse floated by. Rina looked at Frederick, who met her eye. He said, "I wonder if he had children."

Rina didn't answer. Her hand was now rhythmically rubbing circles on her belly. She thought that it was a nice exercise to move furniture, but it was clear to her that this storm wasn't just whipping up trees or wetting rugs. It was taking lives. It wasn't just tearing apart homes; it was ripping apart families.

She thought about her father and her Oma. She thought about her baby. She thought about Haydn. And she started to cry. Frederick took her in his arms.

Down the hall, she heard the sound of shattering glass as something smashed through one of the windows.

"I think everyone will be safer away from the windows," Barton said. "The stairs are probably the safest place."

Everyone moved to the staircase. By the time they settled themselves, water was creeping up onto the lower steps. As it moved up, those sitting on the bottom steps crowded on to the upper stairs.

The inside of the house was now black as night, and the crowding was both a blessing and a curse. The heat of being pressed together was stifling, but knowing that other human beings were still there, that she wasn't alone, was comforting to Rina.

A woman lower down on the stairs began to sing, in an attempt to calm and distract the group. The children joined in, and it seemed that the attempt might be successful, but before the second verse was over, their voices were drowned out by the sound of a window in the living room shattering, followed by the ceaseless shrieking of the wind as it tore through the rooms below them.

Without warning, the water suddenly rose four feet, submerging those sitting on the lowest steps. Everyone grabbed whoever happened to be closest, and they all scrambled up the remaining steps and into second floor rooms. They huddled in corners and on top of furniture trying to stay away from the windows. Then a thudding began.

"What is that banging?" Rina asked. The sound was coming up through the floor, as if something large and angry was beating on the ceiling downstairs.

"It's the furniture," Barton answered. "The piano and other items that we didn't move are floating now and bumping against the ceiling."

The driving rain then began to penetrate the plaster on the walls, creating blisters under the wallpaper that popped like exploding bullets. With each crack, Rina heard children somewhere in the house scream. Then a creaking sound filled the room. Frederick and Rina held hands and looked all around them, trying to peer into the darkness and see where exactly the sound was coming from. Then, with a roar, the roof was ripped off the top of the house, and the storm was upon them.

The wall to the right gave way, and the people who had been leaning against it for shelter, were tossed into the churning water. The wind pulled Rina toward the gaping wound where the wall had been only seconds before, and she fought not to fall into it. In the moonlight, she could see a wall of wreckage, three stories high marching toward them. She heard Frederick shout to her, "When we fall into the water, grab anything you can hold onto to stay afloat!"

She nodded, and soon after, she was in the water. She grabbed a piece of timber that floated by. It was not enough to climb up on, but she could hang her arms over it and keep her head above water. She could see Frederick flailing in the water but could not do anything to help him.

She watched the wall of debris getting closer. It was formed from the houses, buggies, belongings, and people who had once lived on the sand between Barton's home and the beach. Wood snapped like cannon fire from inside it, and Rina thought she could hear screams, but the wind was so loud, she wasn't sure if it was real or her imagination.

She looked away from the wall and back toward where she'd last seen Frederick. She could not see him now, but she saw Barton swimming toward what appeared to be an overturned porch floating toward them. He positioned himself so that he could grab one of the porch's corner posts as it passed, and then he waited for it to come to him. Rina prayed that it would not change course.

She saw another swimmer grab at what used to be the corner of the porch's roof, and it seemed to change the porch's path. Barton screamed, "No!" But then the porch righted itself and continued on its original course, toward him. The swimmer flailed at it, growing more panicked as he was unable to secure it, then as it slipped out of reach, he gave up and clung, exhausted, to a piece of wood.

The porch floated closer and closer, seeming to gather speed. Then, as it almost ran over Barton, he grabbed at the corner post. The porch started to swing around on the current, but he was able to slow it enough for him to jump on it. He then waved at Rina.

She kicked her legs to propel her toward Barton and his porch raft, and the current acquiesced. She was almost to the raft when she heard a cry behind her and saw that it was Barton's youngest boy, Andy. She reached backward and kicked her legs in the opposite direction to try to slow her progress. She managed to grab the collar of Andy's shirt, and she pulled him with her as she floated toward the raft. Barton almost fell out, reaching for her and Andy, then he pulled her up with one hand, grabbing at Andy with the other.

Safely inside the confines of the overturned porch, they felt themselves carried on the tide but could only see what was going on around them when the clouds thinned enough to let the full moon shine through. What Rina saw during these glimpses terrified her.

She saw a landscape largely of emptiness where buildings had once stood, punctuated by the occasional jagged remains of buildings that refused to fall completely. She saw a sea teeming with debris—some human and some not. In the water all around her were people and animals, some alive, some dead, and some she just couldn't tell. She saw some people open their mouths to let the water take them, and she saw others trying with all their might to survive despite being battered with refuse from the storm.

Rina felt herself becoming overwhelmed and forced herself to focus on only one thing—holding onto Andy until the nightmare was over.

CHAPTER 35

SEPTEMBER 8, 1900

The air in Painter House was heavy. When the sun set, with no electric lights to illuminate the night, the entire city was cloaked in utter darkness. Indoors, the blackout was complete. Every door and window was shut tight with pieces of furniture moved in front of them to fortify them, and the wind pounded on the house, throwing unseen missiles at its walls and assaulting the windows. With no fresh air entering the house, and the fear and wounds of wet people filling every room, the atmosphere was choking.

Haydn moved through the house, checking to see if anyone needed anything. After determining that there wasn't much he could do for the guests downstairs, he went upstairs. He found Margaret and Peter huddled on the floor in the hall outside her bedroom.

"Are you okay?" he asked Margaret and knelt down.

"I'm fine," she said. "I'm just tired—tired of death mostly. I don't want any more death," she said and buried her face in Peter's shoulder. Haydn nodded and went back downstairs.

He sat on the floor by the front door, Buddy by his side. He knew it was unlikely anyone else would knock. If anyone was out in the storm now, he didn't see how they could survive, much less make it to the Winters' door. But he wanted to be there just in case.

Melanie came and sat on her knees in front of him. Haydn leaned forward.

"Are you and your husband doing okay?" he asked. "Do you need any medical attention or something to eat?"

"No, we're fine. Thank you," Melanie said. "I like your dog." She stroked Buddy's head.

"He's a good companion. Normally my mother would throw a fit if she saw him inside the house, but I don't imagine she would have an objection right now. And I wouldn't care if she did. It wouldn't be right to leave him out there."

"No, it wouldn't," Melanie said. She took a deep breath, seemed to ponder something, then said, "There's something I think I need to tell you."

Haydn sat back and said, "Okay." Melanie took another breath, then looked him in the eye.

"I'm not sure how all of this is going to end, so I think there's something you deserve to know," she said. "I know how close you and Rina were."

Haydn wondered if she really did know—how much Rina had told her and what any of it could matter now, but he said nothing. She went on.

"I know that you were planning to marry her and that forces beyond your control changed things," she said. Haydn dropped his eyes, feeling a little embarrassed, even though Melanie's tone seemed to hold no judgment. "What you did not know is that things had already changed for Rina."

"Changed how?" Haydn asked, looking back up at her.

"She didn't marry Frederick because she loved him, or because she thought she might end up an old maid after you left her, or for any other reason that people tell themselves when they have been left behind by someone they love." Now Haydn thought he heard an accusation in her voice, but he didn't look away. "She married Frederick because she had to marry someone."

"I don't understand," Haydn said. "What do you mean she 'had' to marry someone?"

Melanie pursed her lips, then leaned in and said as quietly as she could manage over the sound of the storm pounding the house, "She married him for the baby, Mr. Winters. For the baby."

It took a moment for the words to register, then it hit him. If she married him *for* the baby, that means there was already a baby before she was married. His baby.

Euphoria swept through his mind. Rina was having his baby! But then the other reality hit him.

Rina was having his baby. And Frederick was going to be father to the child, not him—provided Frederick and Rina were even still alive, considering what was going on outside. He scrambled to his feet, and Melanie grabbed his arm.

"What are you doing?"

"I must get to her!" he said.

"Are you out of your mind?"

"She's out there with my baby—with our baby! She'll be killed!"

"Haydn, if she's out there, then you're probably right. It's too late. And even if you could get to her, which you couldn't, where would you go? Do you know where she is? Because I don't, and I'm her best friend."

With that, Melanie began to cry. "I would guess she was either at her house or her father's house when things became impassable. And from what I've seen with my own eyes and what I've heard from other people here, that means she's probably gone.

"She wouldn't have left her father and grandmother

to fend for themselves, and I don't see any way that all of them could have gotten to safety unless they left when John and I did, maybe even sooner. There's just not much chance, Haydn."

"No. She can't be gone," he said to himself. Then he looked at Melanie. "She can't be gone! That husband of hers—he would've gotten her to safety, wouldn't he? He wouldn't just let her drown, would he?"

"Frederick loved her very much," she said. "He would've done everything he could for her."

"Don't talk in the past tense," he said angrily.

"I'm sorry," Melanie said. "It's just...you don't know what it's like out there."

He saw her eyes soften as she looked at him. "Look, maybe you're right. Maybe she's still be out there somewhere."

"Then I've got to find her."

"No!" Melanie shouted. "I won't have your death on my hands, and if you go out there because of what I've told you, that's what will happen. Haydn, there is nothing you can do now. This can't last much longer. And besides, it's too dark outside to see anything. Wait until morning. If you want me to go with you to look once it's light, I'll help you."

"I can't do that," Haydn said. "I can't just sit here while the woman I love and our baby may be out there fighting for their lives. If I do nothing, and they die, I'll always wonder if I could've saved them. If that happens, my life won't be worth living." He wrenched open the front door, stepped out on to the porch and the door slammed behind him.

CHAPTER 36

SEPTEMBER 9, 1900

Haydn sat with his back against a tree. His knees were pulled up to his chest, and he rested his head on his arms, folded across his knees. He hadn't made it more than a block or so from his house, but he felt like he'd run a marathon.

When he had run out the door at Painter House, he ran smack into a nightmare. He had struggled to push against the wind and quickly found himself wading through water with legs that felt like lead. He'd felt things scratching across his face and arms, but in the dark, he had no idea what was scratching him, and things large and small had bumped past him in the swirling water.

He'd finally realized he had no clue where to go and

no clue how he could get there. It was all he could do to keep from getting pushed down into the water by the wind. So, he'd stumbled into the closest yard he could find and held on to a tree. By midnight, it was over.

He could see by the moonlight now that the water was receding quickly. He wanted to get up and start searching for Rina, but he knew that until the sun came up, he would be searching blindly. And besides, he had exhausted himself. So, he put his head down and tried to just rest until the sun rose.

Around 3 a.m., he saw some people starting to mill around in the streets. A few hours later, a pink light began to stain the sky. He stood up and looked behind him. The house whose yard he'd invaded was still standing. A cow was standing on the porch. The animal looked at him mournfully but didn't make a sound. Haydn turned and walked into the street.

* * *

Rina and Barton sat up in their raft. The upturned porch had run aground on the massive wall of debris while the storm still raged, and they had decided to stay where they were until morning.

Rina peered over the side of the porch and was greeted with the horrifying site of a woman's body, bobbing in a pool of floodwater that had not yet receded, her hand clutching the lifeless body of a baby. She sat back down.

"I have to go look for the rest of my family," Barton said.

"Of course. I should do the same," Rina said, though she was sure that there would be no one to find. They all sat for a few more seconds to gather their courage, then Barton, Andy, and Rina each climbed over the side of the porch onto the wreckage. Barton looked around for a moment to get his bearings, then took Andy by the hand and began to climb down the mountain of debris into the street.

When Rina reached the street, she realized that she had no idea where to go, so she just picked a direction and started walking. As she surveyed the scene around her, she felt overwhelmed. People wandered around, looking dazed. Some were completely naked, and all were cut, scraped, and bruised. The streets were littered with corpses, and whenever she came close to the wall of wreckage that had scraped the land clean and held their porch through the night, she heard distant screams. She was sure people were alive inside the wall, but didn't know how to get to them.

She walked south, as if to go home—not the home she had shared with Frederick, but the one where she grew up. At Avenue N, though, she stopped. She stared mesmerized. She had a clear view of the Gulf. There was nothing left standing between her and the beach. Everything was gone. That was all she needed to know. Her home was gone, and her father and grandmother were gone.

* * *

Haydn picked his way through the streets. The further south he got, the worse conditions were. It seemed as if every surface was covered in a rancid, greasy slime about an inch deep. Debris, human and otherwise, lay everywhere. A woman approached him wrapped in nothing but a muddy blanket.

"Have you seen my children? Adelaide and Christopher?" she asked him mechanically.

He didn't know the woman, much less her children.

"No, ma'am, I'm sorry." She walked away, and he heard her ask again to no one in particular.

The destruction was staggering. He saw houses tipped at precarious angles, the shutters ripped away, held in place by the remains of other houses. Lumber, stone and metal, torn and twisted covered the streets. He picked his way to the shore to find the beach a graveyard of battered sailing vessels.

After several hours, his mind numbing to so much ghastly devastation, he finally saw her. Rina was in a field of bricks, moving large, heavy blocks with her bare hands.

Her hair was a jumble. Her clothes were ripped. But it was her.

"Rina!" he screamed and began to scramble across the blocks. She turned toward the sound of his voice. Her face was streaked with tears, and when she saw him, her face seem to simultaneously light up and fall.

"Oh Haydn. Is that really you?"

When he got to her, he threw his arms around her. She dropped the bricks in her hands and hugged him back.

"I'm so sorry," he said, burying his face in her tangled hair.

"For what?" Rina asked.

"For taking so long," he said. "For everything."

When they finally released their embrace, Haydn looked down, and he saw what Rina had been doing before he ran up to her. In front of her, partially covered, but fully dead, was her husband.

"Oh, Rina," he said.

Rina looked back at Frederick, and Haydn saw tears start to fill her eyes again. She reached down to lift a brick off of Frederick's body, and Haydn could see that her hands were raw. Haydn leaned down and started tossing away bricks.

The two worked together until they had freed Frederick's body from the wreckage. Haydn then lifted the sodden, heavy corpse and stumbled across the bricks to the street.

"Where shall we take him?" he asked her.

He saw her struggle for a moment with an answer, looking around, then she finally pointed toward the beach and said, "The dunes."

Haydn wasn't sure what would be left of the dunes after such high winds and waves, but he walked toward the beach anyway.

They took Frederick to a clear spot, dug a shallow grave with their hands, then covered him with sand, mounding it up. Haydn was sure the grave would not last. Most likely, it would be blown open by wind or dug up by animals. But it was what Rina wanted, so for now, it would have to do.

When they were done, they stood up and Rina bowed her head. Haydn did the same, though at the moment, he was too exhausted to think of a prayer. So, he just waited for Rina to finish whatever conversation she was having with God.

After a few moments, she lifted her head, and they looked at one another. He could see that she was as tired as he was, but there was something else. She looked like she wanted to say something, but the words wouldn't come. He swept a lock of hair from her eyes.

"Melanie told me," he said. She searched his face for a moment without saying anything. He placed his hand softly on her belly, then smiled at her.

Relief spread across her face, and he heard her exhale. She nodded, and a small smile spread across her lips. She pressed her head into his chest, then stepped back and looked him in the eye.

"Well, then," she said. "What now?"

He embraced her, and they held each other for a long time. When they pulled apart, he took her hand. "Let's go home."

POSTLOGUE

A WORD FROM THE AUTHOR

The Galveston hurricane of 1900 stands to this day as the deadliest natural disaster in United States history. The final death toll is generally accepted to be about 6,000 people, though some estimates put it as high as 8,000.

Galveston, once known as "The Wall Street of the West" never fully recovered. The city did its best to rebound as quickly as possible. By Wednesday, September 12, mail was arriving again, and merchants opened for business to sell goods, though many of the canned goods no longer had labels. On Thursday, September 13, the Galveston *Daily News* printed a full-size paper and telegraph lines were functioning again. And by Friday,

September 14, banks were open again.

But it took months to clear away the wreckage and find all the bodies. In fact, beachgoers on the mainland still stumbled upon the skeletons of victims years later.

After the storm, the city undertook two ambitious projects to make the city safer. The first was a seawall. In 1902, the city contracted to build a six-mile, reinforced concrete seawall, 16-feet thick at the base, rising 17 feet above low tide and fronted by granite blocks. The wall was completed in 1904 and proved its worth in 1915 when another hurricane, almost as powerful as the 1900 storm, struck the city. This time, only 12 lives were lost.

The second project was a grade rising for the island. The city was literally raised by lifting more than 2,000 buildings and infrastructure, such as water pipes and streetcar trestles, with jacks and pilings and pumping sand from the bottom of the Gulf and depositing it underneath them. Using this method, the city was raised to almost 17 feet near the seawall and sloped downward gradually from there to the north. This monumental project was completed in 1910.

While Galveston was figuring out how to survive into the 20th century, though, Houston usurped its position as the premier port and center of commerce for the state of Texas. Galveston never regained its prominent position, though it experienced a renaissance by the end of the century, as private investors, mainly the

Moody family, restored and renovated many of the historic buildings in the city, including a large stretch of the Strand district.

Not only was much of the early flavor of the island restored, but many new attractions, such as the Moody Gardens Hotel and Spa Resort, were built, helping to increase tourism and make Galveston once again a resort destination. The city revived its annual Mardi Gras celebration, and it hosts Dickens on The Strand, a Victorian Christmas celebration, each December.

But Galveston will never forget the events of September 8, 1900. On September 8, 2000, the 100-year anniversary of the storm, a memorial to the victims of the storm was dedicated. The statue, "A Place of Remembrance," sits on the seawall, which still stands sentinel for the city, at 48th street. The 10-foot tall bronze sculpture depicts a father, mother, and child, clinging together, the father's arm raised to the heavens forever.

On September 13, 2008, Galveston was again battered by a major hurricane. Hurricane Ike roared across the city with Category 2 winds and massive flooding. It caused widespread devastation and destroyed many of the structures and landmarks across the island. Loss of life was minimal, however—approximately 23 people in the entire state—thanks to a mandatory evacuation of the island, ignored by some. The memorial to the 1900 victims withstood the storm.

ACKNOWLEDGMENTS

Thank you so much to the people who helped me with this incredible project. I could not have created this work without the assistance of the wonderful people at the Rosenberg Library in Galveston; the encouragement of my incredible husband Jonathan Thelin; and the time and efforts donated by friends and family, including the always supportive Sheila Shoff. I extend special thanks to Sara Kocek and Ashley Kraft. Your invaluable editing skills made all the difference to me and to this novel. Thank you, thank you, thank you!

Overflow

ABOUT THE AUTHOR

Suzanne Staton is a writer, editor, musician, and beach lover. A graduate of The University of Texas at Austin with degrees in English and journalism, she's worked professionally as a writer, editor, columnist, and freelance communications consultant. A lifelong Texan, she grew up going to the beach in Galveston and still visits the island frequently. She lives in Central Texas with her husband.

www.ingramcontent.com/pod-product-compliance
Lightning Source LLC
Chambersburg PA
CBHW051336250626
47155CB00007B/2616